A Test *of* Love

A Test of Love

KATHLEEN SCOTT

Grand Rapids, MI 49501

A Test of Love

Published by Kregel Publications, a division of Kregel, Inc., P.O. Box 2607, Grand Rapids, MI 49501. For more information about Kregel Publications, visit our Web site: www.kregel.com.

Cover design: John M. Lucas

ISBN 0-8254-3664-8

Printed in the United States of America

2 3 4 5 / 06 05 04 03 02

"[Love] always protects, always trusts, always hopes, always perseveres. Love never fails."

1 Corinthians 13:7–8a

Chapter One

Juliet Nelson looked at herself in the dressing room mirror at Victoria's Secret and felt like a fool. She could not take comfort in the realization that teaching aerobics classes for the past year had done marvelous things for her figure. All she noticed was that she was not the kind of woman who could look comfortable in a black lace teddy. This was simply not her style. She loved coming to this shop. The elegant, feminine decorations, the scents of perfume and potpourri, and the soft classical music made it one of her favorite places in the mall. But she just would have been happier trying on a pretty and modest cotton nightgown. Desperation was pushing Juliet out of her comfort zone.

After eleven years of marriage, she and Michael were in trouble. If you'd asked Michael how married life was going, he would have told you that it was wonderful. Fantastic. He didn't seem to comprehend how miserable Juliet had become over the years as she watched the romance in their relationship slowly die. These days Juliet felt as though they lived like friendly roommates instead of devoted lovers, and she was determined to bring the excitement back. She sighed and changed back into her jeans and black cotton sweater. She might feel ridiculous in the teddy, but she would just have to perform the acting job of her life tonight. Michael was worth it. More than anything, she wanted to have a marriage that was alive and passionate.

As Juliet drove north on Highway 1 back toward Mount Hermon, California, she wondered how she and Michael had gotten to such a complacent spot in their marriage. It wasn't due to a lack of interest or effort on Juliet's part. Over the years, she had read books and magazine articles that promised readers new levels of excitement in their relationships just by using a few simple ideas. She must have tried more than a dozen of them. She'd tucked little love notes in Michael's briefcase, given him back and foot massages by candlelight, and lovingly prepared picnics for two in front of their bedroom fireplace after the children had been put to bed for the night. She'd also made more bold attempts at seduction, like the time she'd met Michael in the garage one night after work, wearing a raincoat and nothing else. Michael usually met her efforts with halfhearted appreciation, as if he didn't want to hurt her feelings but simply couldn't get excited about her plans.

Her most ambitious romantic endeavor had taken place last January, right after their eleventh wedding anniversary. Juliet had secretly made reservations for a weekend at a cozy bed-and-breakfast at San Luis Obispo that her friend Sally Day had told her about. Their room was perfect, with a window seat overlooking the Pacific Ocean, a fireplace, and a sunken whirlpool bathtub. Juliet had arranged for Sally to keep their two daughters, Daisy and Heather, for the two nights. She had even plotted with Michael's secretary at Redwood Real Estate to reschedule his weekend appointments. Juliet showed up at his office in Felton that Friday afternoon with their bags packed and insisted that he get in the car with her.

As they drove down the mountain toward Santa Cruz, she began to wonder if her idea had been completely wrong. Michael seemed anything but happy about her plans to kidnap him for the weekend. All he could talk about was the serious customer who had seemed ready and eager to buy. He was obviously angry with her for rescheduling his appointments. "A good salesman doesn't put off a hot customer, Juliet. You know that most of my customers aren't free to look at real estate during the week."

Juliet insisted that their marriage needed attention occasionally, and they went on to San Luis Obispo. He never was able to relax and enjoy what could have been a perfect weekend in a gorgeous setting because he was so preoccupied with the work he was missing. On the drive home, he made her promise that she would never reschedule his work for a surprise trip out of town again.

The customer was still interested when Michael got back

to the office, and he bought a house within the week. It all worked out wonderfully; it usually did for Michael. He had been named a top real estate agent so many times that Juliet had lost count. Of course, she was truly thankful for his dedication to providing for her and their girls, and she loved their home. It was more than she'd ever dreamed she would have, growing up in a modest townhouse in San Jose.

Leonard Kendrick, Juliet's father, was an English professor at San Jose State University. His two passions were the works of Shakespeare and his wife. To Juliet and her older sister, Jessica, it seemed that their parents had a love that nothing could diminish. Juliet could still remember the excitement in her mother's voice when she would call up the stairs, "Girls! Daddy's home!" Then they would hear her rush into the downstairs powder room for a touch-up of her lipstick, a quick fluffing of her hair, and a light misting of Chanel No. 5. As Juliet's dad came through the doorway, her mother would meet him with a passionate embrace and prolonged kiss, while Jessica and Juliet watched and giggled from the top of the stairs. When Mom was done greeting Dad, the girls knew they'd get their hugs. Leonard Kendrick adored his "little ladies," as he lovingly referred to his daughters. They just knew that Mommy came first, and it made them happy to see how much their parents loved each other.

Marie Kendrick died when Juliet was fifteen and Jessica was attending UC Davis. Leonard was devastated by his loss and had never found another woman to love. Juliet promised herself that someday she would have a beautiful relationship just like the one her parents had shared. But she never imagined it would take so much effort on her part.

Juliet glanced at her watch as she stood in the long checkout line, with a cart full of groceries and a bouquet of gold and yellow chrysanthemums and daisies. She planned to surprise Michael by making him a romantic steak dinner for two. Their little girls were away at a sleepover with Sally's daughter, Katie. Juliet was running out of time, but she took comfort in knowing that the grocery store was just minutes from their house. For once, the fact that Michael never left the office at five o'clock would work in her favor.

The house was completely dark as Juliet parked her Cadillac in the garage. It was only the end of September, but already the days were short and the nights were damp and chilly. "Just a minute, Heathcliff." Juliet opened the kitchen door and was met with exuberant jumps and kisses from her Border collie. "Let's hope Daddy is as thrilled to see me tonight as you are. Oh, I missed you too, Heathcliff! Where's Sheba? I've got to feed you guys and get dinner going. Everything has to be ready when Daddy gets here."

As she turned on the kitchen lights, she felt a gentle rubbing against her legs and looked down to see the sweet, white, Persian face of her cat, Sheba. Juliet fed her some of her favorite gourmet salmon cat food on the kitchen countertop then put some mesquite marinade on the rib-eye steaks. Then she arranged the flowers and candles on the old oak kitchen table, got a fire going in the kitchen fireplace, dimmed the lights, and turned on the soft, instrumental music that Michael preferred.

She was upstairs putting on satin lounging pajamas, the same stormy-blue color as her eyes, when she heard Michael come in the front door. She pulled her dark hair back with a blue satin ribbon and ran down the stairs. He was looking through a stack of mail and didn't notice Juliet watching him. It amazed her that after all these years, the sight of Michael could still put butterflies in her stomach. He was everything that appealed to her in a man—tall, rugged, yet sophisticated. He looked as though he'd be just as comfortable leading a business meeting as he would building a deck on the back of a house. The afternoons they had spent at the pool last summer had left him with some golden highlights in his sandy brown hair. And at the age of forty-two, he only looked more manly and handsome to Juliet with the slight wrinkling around his hazel eyes and the weathering of his skin.

"Hi, honey! How was your day?"

"Great! Where are the girls?" Michael asked, without taking his eyes from the mail.

Juliet kissed his cheek, savoring the smell of English Leather as she whispered in his ear, "They're at Sally's tonight. We have the whole house to ourselves. I'm just about to put steaks on the grill. Want to come out on the deck and keep me company while I cook them?"

"First I've got to make a quick phone call; I'm trying to set something up for tomorrow morning."

"Oh, Michael, the girls are staying with the Days until tomorrow night. I was hoping we could spend the morning together." Juliet tried unsuccessfully to keep the disappointment she felt out of her voice.

"Sweetheart, you know Saturdays are always booked for me. I'll make the call and bring you out some iced tea."

Juliet stood outside on the back deck, watching the steaks sizzle on the grill, waiting for Michael to bring out the promised iced tea, and wishing she'd put on a jacket. It didn't surprise her that Michael wasn't willing to give up a day of work to spend time with her. Well, they still had tonight, and she was going to make the most of it. But the steaks were cooked to medium rare—the way Michael liked them—before he ever remembered to come outside with her tea. She turned off the gas grill and went inside to finish setting the table next to the cheerful kitchen fireplace.

Juliet called Michael to dinner for the third time, with a threat that his steak would be cold. Finally he got off the phone, hurried to the kitchen, and sat down across the antique table from her. "This looks great," he said with a smile.

"Did I tell you that my sister called yesterday and is trying to set things up so that we can all spend Thanksgiving together at her in-laws' cabin at Lake Tahoe?"

"How long would we be gone?" Michael asked skeptically.

"Jessie and I want to get there by Wednesday night, so that we'll be all settled in and ready to start cooking on Thanksgiving morning."

"Do you plan to be gone the whole weekend?"

"Sure. That's the nice part about going out of town for the Thanksgiving weekend. You can have a four-day holiday without taking any time from work."

"Maybe for Jessica and Dan, they're teachers. I don't get four days off."

"You weren't planning to work that weekend, were you?" She couldn't believe what she was hearing. In the early years of their marriage, Michael might occasionally work on a Saturday for a few hours, but never on Sunday or during the holidays. "Even you planned to take Thanksgiving off, I hope. Who shops for houses over the holiday weekend?"

"I do—if someone is interested."

"Michael, we haven't taken a vacation with our girls for the past two summers. I think you can afford to spend a long Thanksgiving weekend with your children." It was time to change the subject. This topic was making her feel angry and frustrated. Tonight was supposed to be happy, relaxing, and above all, romantic. Getting into an argument would not help her meet those goals.

After dinner, Juliet straightened up the kitchen and ran upstairs to get a bubble bath going in their whirlpool tub. She lit more candles, put on the black lace teddy, and looked in the full-length mirror on her closet door. The effect was dramatic, with her long black hair nearly as dark as the lingerie, and she wondered why it didn't look right on her. She supposed that women who enjoyed wearing such outfits had a lot of confidence in their sex appeal. That was something Juliet definitely did not have.

Sheba came purring into the room and settled into her evening sleeping spot on the white love seat in front of the bedroom fireplace. Juliet thought about lighting a fire but was afraid of taking any longer to go back to Michael. He didn't like to stay up very late, and she had already taken a long time cleaning up after dinner and preparing the bath.

"Here goes nothing. Wish me luck, Sheba." She looked in the mirror one last time, took a deep breath, and went to find Michael. He was in the living room, stretched out on his favorite recliner, watching an old *Star Trek* rerun. She sat on his lap and said in a voice that she hoped was seductive, "Honey, I have a bubble bath ready upstairs for us."

"Is that a new outfit? Aren't you a little cold? This is one of my favorite episodes. I'll come up later, but I'm not really in the mood for a bath." He barely took his eyes from the television screen, even though she knew he had seen that particular episode at least three times. *Star Trek* was a real bone of contention between them. She hated the show, and it came on right when they put Daisy and Heather to bed. So when the house could have been quiet for them to share their hearts at the end of the day,

Michael was watching dumb reruns instead. He insisted that he loved the show and watching it helped him unwind after a hard day.

Juliet got off his lap with her face turned away so he wouldn't see how upset and embarrassed she felt. She went upstairs, got into the bath alone, took off her makeup, and let the tears of anger and disappointment come. She told herself she was a stupid fool to set herself up for rejection time after time. She had tried everything she could to make Michael interested in their love life. Nothing had worked. She was out of ideas and worn out emotionally from her efforts.

When the water started to grow cool, she stepped out of the bath, drained the tub while she dried herself off, then went into her room and shoved the teddy to the back of her lingerie drawer. She pulled a comfortable, old, blue-flowered cotton nightgown over her head. As she brushed her hair in front of the dresser mirror, she looked at their bedroom, so beautifully decorated in shades of blue and white. Years before, when Daisy was a baby, she and Michael had spared no expense to completely redecorate this room. They had put a lot of time and thought into designing their own love nest, as they had liked to call it. Now the impressive four-poster bed and velveteen-and-satin comforter seemed to mock her with its sensual opulence. Nothing exciting had happened in this room for a long time. She put down the hairbrush and crawled into bed next to her faithful Heathcliff, who had already warmed a spot for her.

Chapter Two

Juliet opened her eyes the next morning and simultaneously noticed that it was nine o'clock and that Michael had already left for the office. Heathcliff was whining to go outside, so she reluctantly pushed the down comforter away and got out of bed.

In the kitchen, while she fixed some coffee and a bowl of granola, she toyed with the idea of calling Sally and asking to spend the day with the girls. She just as quickly dismissed that idea; Sally would guess that something had gone wrong with her romantic weekend plans. And as close as Juliet was to Sally, the discouragement she felt about her marriage was not a subject she would willingly discuss with anyone. She decided that a long walk in the woods and some quiet time to read and think would be the best way to spend her day off from motherhood. She dressed in some comfortable worn-out jeans, a turtleneck, an old sweater, and hiking boots. Then she stuffed her backpack with a thick cotton blanket, the mystery novel she was halfway through, a thermos of hot tea, and a sandwich of cream cheese and green olives.

Juliet found Heathcliff waiting for her in the front yard. When she headed down the sidewalk toward the road and called to him, he began to leap and run in circles around her. Fall and spring were Juliet's favorite seasons at Mount Hermon. Winter was usually damp and dreary, and living near the Christian retreat center during the busy summer season was sometimes frustrating. After Memorial Day, the normally quiet and sleepy community suddenly became overrun with visitors on vacation. They created traffic jams and filled up the parking lot in front of the little neighborhood post office. Then Labor Day arrived and everything became peaceful again. Truly, there was never a season that Juliet wasn't thankful to live in such a unique and beautiful place. Who could blame the crowds of conference goers, wanting to have a little taste of the heaven on earth that she got to enjoy all year round?

Heathcliff and Juliet hiked together on the steep, narrow trail that led down from the conference center to the boat dock and swimming pool. The path was dark and cool even on the hottest days of summer because of all the magnificent redwood trees that towered over the forest. Equally huge eucalyptus trees along the worn, dirt paths filled the air with the scent of menthol.

As she followed her dog through the woods, Juliet was flooded with memories of her first visit to Mount Hermon and her immediate love for the place. Her mother had died of cancer during the spring of Juliet's sophomore year in high school. That summer, a friend invited Juliet to go to camp for a week in August with the youth group from church. Leonard Kendrick thought that some time in the mountains would be therapeutic for his daughter after the ordeal their family had just gone through, and he sent her with his blessing.

Every summer after that, Juliet had gotten live-in positions at the retreat center; first working in the day-care center, then as a waitress the following year, and finally settling into her favorite job as a lifeguard. Those summers provided a refreshing break for her, after going to school in the hectic and crowded San Jose area and keeping house for her father. Even after she started attending San Jose State University, she still worked at Mount Hermon every summer and dreaded the last days of August when she knew it was almost over for another year. After so many years, the place still looked the same, still held the same charm.

Eventually, Juliet and her dog hiked back to the ballpark next to their house. She spread out the picnic blanket, and Heathcliff stretched out in the sun next to her to take a nap. Juliet smiled as she remembered sunbathing in that exact spot the day she'd met Michael.

Juliet and Carrie, her roommate that summer, had been given the afternoon off and decided to work on their tans.

Juliet didn't want to go back to the pool—she had taught swim classes there all morning—so they decided to take their books to the huge, grassy ball field next to the administration office. It was June, and some boys were playing Little League baseball on the field. Juliet was caught up in the final chapters of a romance novel and completely ignored the game until a fly ball hit her on the head. She sat up on her old blanket, rubbing her temple and trying not to cry. Suddenly, a long shadow fell across her, and she looked up into the face of Michael Nelson.

"I am so sorry. Are you okay? Here, let me feel that bump on your head. You may have a concussion."

"Oh, I'm sure I'll be fine. Your kids sure know how to hit that ball," she said in a feeble attempt to make a joke.

"I'm not so sure. Please let me take you over to the urgent care center."

"Well, we have a first-aid office right next door. I work here, and it wouldn't cost anything."

"Okay, I'll take you there right now."

Michael obviously wouldn't take no for an answer, and Juliet's head was hurting too much to argue with him. The nurse checked her out, gave her some Tylenol for her headache, and said she'd probably be fine but suggested that she stay with someone for the next twelve hours to make sure she didn't fall asleep unexpectedly or display any other symptoms of severe head injury.

As they were leaving the first-aid office, Michael asked Juliet if she would go out to dinner with him. "It's the least I can do after ruining your day off."

"Don't you have to go back and get your little boy from the ball game?"

"I don't have any kids. A guy from my office has a son on the team, and I like to coach. It's fun to watch those little guys learn the game."

"Well, actually I'm not doing anything special tonight. I just need to check back with my roommate to let her know I'm okay. Can I meet you in front of the bookstore at the conference center in about an hour? I'd like to take a shower and change my clothes."

"Maybe we should make it an hour and a half so that I'll have time to go home and change, too." He looked at his watch. "I'll meet you at seven o'clock at the bookstore, and you'd better be on time or I'll come looking for you to make sure you haven't slipped into a coma somewhere."

Juliet promised she'd be there and walked away giggling. She wondered if she was feeling dizzy from the bump on her head or from the realization that she was going out to dinner with the most handsome man she had ever met.

She burst through the door of the cabin she shared with Carrie and launched into a nonstop monologue of all that had happened since the ball had hit her. "And he insisted that I have dinner with him tonight; he refused to take no for an answer! He is such a confident, take-charge kind of guy. I'm going to meet him at seven o'clock which means . . . oh my gosh! I have less than an hour to get ready! Oh, Carrie, did you notice how gorgeous he is?"

"Yes," Carrie lamented. "Why is it that all the neatest things happen to you, Juliet? Why didn't that baseball land twelve inches to the right and hit my head instead? That guy is definitely one of the cutest California hunks I have ever seen."

"Well, I'm not going to let myself get carried away. Did you see how much older he looked? He probably just feels sorry for me and sees me as some kid that he should be nice to, like the little kids he coaches. Funny thing is, I feel absolutely great and kind of guilty for letting him take me out to dinner because of some little bump on my head."

"I'm sure he doesn't see you as one of his Little League kids, Juliet. Give me a break! I saw the way he looked at you. You'll probably be engaged by the end of the summer. Just make sure he's a Christian first."

"What an imagination you have, Carrie. I wouldn't be surprised if he was a Christian though. Isn't it sweet that he coaches those little boys and doesn't even have a child of his own?"

A short while later, Juliet glanced at her bedside alarm clock as she rushed out the door of the cabin. It was already ten minutes after seven. She chided herself for taking so long to choose a dress to wear. She had tried on four different outfits and finally chosen a simple white sleeveless dress that showed off her tan. From the look on Michael's face when she reached the bookstore, she decided she had made the right choice.

"I'm sorry I'm late. Have you been waiting very long?"

"I would have been happy to wait all night to take out such a pretty girl." Michael smiled at her as she blushed and felt her heart race. "Glad to see you aren't lying unconscious somewhere."

"Actually, I feel guilty letting you take me to dinner. I'm sure I don't have a concussion, and this seems like a lot of fuss over nothing."

"What this is, Juliet, is a great excuse for a lonely guy to take a beautiful girl out to dinner."

"You know, I never dreamed getting hit on the head could be such a delightful experience." She grinned and tucked her hand around the arm he held out for her.

They got into his white BMW and headed toward the Santa Cruz Yacht Harbor and the Crow's Nest, his favorite restaurant. The maitre d' immediately led them to a table at a window overlooking the Pacific Ocean, in spite of the crowd of people waiting at the front of the restaurant. Juliet was surprised to get such special treatment and asked Michael how he'd managed to get them a table so quickly. "I often bring my house-hunting customers here, so they know me pretty well." Then he grinned at her over the top of his menu. "But the real secret is, I called ahead from my apartment."

After the waitress had taken their order, Juliet noticed that Michael was staring at her, and she blushed under his scrutiny.

"Are you checking to see if my pupils are dilated? I guess that's a sign of a concussion, but honestly I feel completely fine."

"No. I'm trying to think of what color I would use to describe your eyes. I don't think I've ever seen eyes like yours before. It's like looking into the deep end of a swimming pool. It's mesmerizing."

"Thank you. I inherited them from my mom."

"Do your parents live around here?"

"No, my mother died of cancer when I was fifteen, and my dad lives in San Jose. He's an English professor at San Jose State. I live there with him when I'm going to school."

"You didn't want to move into the dorms and get away from home?"

"When Mom died, I was the only one left with Dad. I have an older sister, but she was living in the dorms at UC Davis. Dad and I got so close during my last two years in high school after Mom was gone, I couldn't leave him. He is such a wonderful man. And he was such a lousy cook, he probably would have tried to live on sandwiches and cereal and would have starved to death."

"That's not much of a life for a teenager," Michael replied, looking at her intently. "Did it bother you to have to take on so much responsibility when you were so young?"

"Well, I've come here every summer since I was fifteen. During the summers, I've lived like every other kid. I've been very happy with my life. Dad is a lot of fun to live with. And he's learned how to cook, so I don't have to feel guilty when I leave for the summer."

Michael told Juliet a little bit about his background, and she was amazed that someone so young could have made such a success of himself. He was only ten years older than she, but he had started selling real estate after he graduated from UC Santa Cruz and had done extremely well.

As they walked along the beach after dinner, Juliet took

a deep breath and asked him the question she'd known all evening she would have to raise. "Do you go to church anywhere around here?"

"When I was a kid, my parents used to make sure I went with them to Seaside Bible Church every Sunday. I haven't been very faithful about going in the past few years, now that I live by myself. It seems that most Sundays I either have an appointment to show some property or I'm sleeping in. How about you? I guess you have to be a Christian to work at a Christian retreat center."

"I can't imagine how I would have survived the death of my mother if I hadn't known that I'd see her again someday in heaven. Spending so many summers with Christian friends has really helped my faith grow and become the most important thing in my life."

"Well, you've convinced me. I promise to be in church bright and early this Sunday, that is, if you'll come with me and let me take you out to lunch afterward."

"I'd love to go with you, Michael. But it will have to be a quick lunch. I'm lifeguarding Sunday afternoon."

That set the pattern for the rest of the summer. Juliet worked during the day and went out with Michael several nights each week. They had a standing date to go to church and brunch every Sunday, and by the beginning of August, they were both dreading the changes that would occur when she went back to San Jose.

Juliet had never known a man like Michael. She hadn't dated very much in her twenty years. A few guys had taken her out, but it was never anything serious. Now she realized that, compared to Michael, they were boys. He was so mature and confident, yet she could be silly with him and talk to him about anything. She had never dated anyone who made her feel so special. Michael treated her like a delicate porcelain doll. Often he sent her flowers or a cute card for no special reason, or he'd bring a pink rose for her when he came to take her out on a date. He had discovered early in their friendship that pink roses were her favorite. It was like him to remember details like that.

A growl in her stomach brought Juliet back to the present. She sat up on the picnic blanket and looked across the ballpark at her house. She took out her sandwich, broke off a corner of it to feed to Heathcliff, and poured some tea from the thermos. From the first time she had come to Mount Hermon, that house had always been her favorite. The large, two-story house was painted robin's egg blue with white trim. A big deck off the back overlooked the ballpark, and huge redwood trees provided plenty of shade.

On one of Michael and Juliet's first dates, they had hiked around the Mount Hermon neighborhood, and she had pointed out the house to him. "Isn't it gorgeous, Michael? Someday I'd like to live in a place just like that."

"I know what you mean. We lived in town in a shoebox tract home when I was growing up. I've always wanted to raise my kids in a neighborhood like this, in a big house, with lots of room to run."

One August evening on Juliet's twenty-first birthday and about five days before she was due to go back to San Jose and college, Michael came to pick her up for a dinner date. Instead of going to where his car was parked, he took Juliet's hand and asked her to go for a walk with him. They headed toward her favorite house, and he surprised her by leading her up the walkway to the front door.

"What are we doing? I didn't think you knew the people who live here."

Michael pulled out a set of keys and found the one for the front door. "Well, at the moment, nobody lives here. I've been asked to sell this house for Mr. and Mrs. Murray. I thought you'd like to see the inside of your favorite Mount Hermon house."

"Oh, Michael! This is the greatest birthday surprise. Thank you. I've always wondered what the inside was like."

He put his hand on the small of her back as she walked through the front door. "Juliet, this is one of the things I love about you. You are so easy to please and surprise."

As they wandered from room to room, Juliet realized that this truly was the house of her dreams. French doors led to the deck out back, and lovely tiled fireplaces provided dramatic focal points in several rooms. Even the wallpaper and carpeting were what she would have chosen. "This is so beautiful. Why would they ever sell it?"

"Mr. Murray has been transferred to Florida, otherwise I doubt that they would have given it up. They lived here for fourteen years."

"And Mrs. Murray either has a natural talent for decorating

or hired an interior decorator, because this place is perfect. I'm sure you'll have no trouble selling it."

"Actually, an offer has already been made on it. Sweetheart, there's something I need to talk to you about." Michael led her to the stairway going up from the living room and sat her down on the steps. Then he knelt in front of her and took her hand.

"Juliet, I've been looking for a girl like you all my life. I've made an offer on this house, but I only want to live here if you'll come with me and be my wife." He pulled out a small black velvet box and opened it to remove an oval sapphire ring surrounded by tiny diamonds. When he put it on the ring finger of her left hand, it fit perfectly.

Juliet was too shocked to take it in all at once—the man of her dreams and the house of her dreams. Dazed, she was sure that she must have heard him incorrectly. "What are you saying, Michael?"

"Juliet, I love you. I'm asking you to marry me and live happily ever after in this beautiful house."

Chapter Three

The rest of that year passed in a happy blur. Michael took Juliet back to San Jose and helped her break the news to her dad that he was losing his other daughter. Jessica had married Dan Parker, a fellow student from UC Davis, two years earlier, and they both worked as teachers in Scott's Valley. Juliet had taken Michael over to visit Jessica and Dan a couple times during the summer, and they were delighted when Michael told them that Juliet had agreed to marry him.

They decided to have a candlelit evening wedding in January at the chapel in Mount Hermon, with a dinner afterward at Chaminade, a lovely hotel overlooking the Santa Cruz Bay. Juliet asked Jessica to be her matron of honor, and Michael's best friend and former college roommate, Bill, agreed to be his best man.

Those autumn months were busy and exciting for Juliet,

as she took more classes toward completing her physical education degree and shopped for the wedding and her future home. She seemed to spend half of her time in her old, beat-up Toyota, driving over Highway 17 to take classes in San Jose and then going back to Santa Cruz to plan the wedding with Jessica and help Michael get their house ready.

Late on Christmas morning, Juliet's father sat down on the side of her bed with a glass of orange juice in his hand. "Hey, sleepyhead. Are you going to wake up today?"

"Hi, Dad. Merry Christmas." Juliet sat up in bed and squinted at the alarm clock. She took the glass of juice and drank it in two big gulps. "Thanks. I guess I stayed up too late wrapping presents." She had gone to a candlelit Christmas Eve service with Michael the night before and then had stayed up wrapping gifts. For Michael, Juliet had chosen a leather jacket he had admired when they were out Christmas shopping together one afternoon, and she was eager to give it to him.

"Do you realize that this will be our last Christmas together?" Her dad's words and the tender look on his face caused Juliet's eyes to fill with tears.

"Oh, Dad, are you sorry that I'm marrying Michael?"

"Of course not! Michael is going to be a wonderful husband for you. It's plain to see that he adores you. Did you know that from the time you and Jessica were little girls—my 'little ladies'—I've been praying that God would send the right men to become your husbands? I think Michael is God's choice for you."

Juliet reached over and hugged her father. "Thank you

for praying for me all those years, Dad. But now you'll be all alone. . . ." She could no longer hold back the tears, and she hugged her dad tighter as she cried on his shoulder.

Leonard hugged his daughter and stroked her hair as he gently asked, "Are you happy that you're going to be a married woman soon?"

"Oh yes!" She sat up straight and smiled at him through her tears. "Michael is everything I've always hoped for in a husband."

"Then that's all that matters, honey. You've been worrying about me and taking care of me and this house for years now. It's time for you to find your own happiness and build your own life with someone you love. It's not like you're moving to another country; I'm sure we'll still see each other often."

The doorbell rang, and Leonard and Juliet looked at one another quizzically. "Are you expecting someone, Juliet?" he asked as he left to see who was at the door.

A moment later, Leonard reappeared at Juliet's bedroom door and told her that someone wanted to see her downstairs. He smiled mysteriously at her questions and refused to tell her who it was. Finally, she pulled on her old, blue, terry cloth robe, splashed some cold water on her face, and decided that whoever it was would have to see her with no makeup.

Hurrying down the stairs, she found Michael in the living room, drinking coffee with her dad. "Hi, honey! What's going on? I thought we weren't going to see you till this afternoon at Jessie's."

"Well, it's Christmas, and I didn't want to wait that long to see my bride-to-be." He pulled her into his arms for a long hug and a kiss, while Leonard politely left the room to fix a mug of coffee for Juliet. "Actually, I wanted to do more than kiss you. I have a Christmas gift that was a little hard to wrap, and your dad tells me you're the gift-wrapping expert in your family."

"I guess I have become pretty good at it over the years. What do you need to have wrapped?"

"It's kind of big—I couldn't bring it inside. Here, let me show you." He opened the front door and led her out to the street in front of their townhouse. A new, dark-blue Honda Accord sat parked by the curb. "Merry Christmas, sweetheart."

"You're not serious, are you? Michael, how could you get me a new car for Christmas? You just bought us a new house! Will we be able to afford it? I'm stunned. I just got you a normal, regular gift, and you bought me a car? I don't know what to say."

"Do you like it?"

"Oh, Michael, you know I love it! I've always wanted a car like this. I'm just in shock."

"Don't worry. We can afford it. I sold that huge place on the coast last week. Besides, I've been worried that if you don't get a better car, you may not make it until our wedding. That old junker of yours is a death trap. I didn't think you'd want me to special order one in the color of your favorite pink roses, so I got one the color of your eyes instead."

"Oh, honey, forgive me for not thanking you properly. You are the most amazing person I've ever known. I never know what you're going to do next. And I'm so glad you didn't get me a pink car. This is absolutely perfect."

Michael opened the passenger door and pulled out a bouquet of long-stemmed pink roses, and she saw that the keys to the car hung from the big satin bow tied around their stems. They went back inside together to have some coffee and enjoy the Kendricks' traditional Christmas morning cinnamon rolls.

Before Juliet realized it, the day before her wedding had arrived. She and her father planned to stay overnight with Jessica and Dan after the rehearsal dinner to save having to make another trip back and forth from San Jose. That morning as she packed the clothes she'd be taking on her honeymoon, Juliet felt bittersweet. This was the only home she had ever lived in, and all of her memories of her mother and her childhood were wrapped up within its walls. She was thrilled to look forward to living with Michael in their new home, but it would be hard to leave her dad.

She had talked to Michael about how concerned she was about leaving her dad alone. "I'd feel so much better if he had someone special in his life. At least a lady who he would enjoy eating dinner with now and then. Friends of his have introduced him to women over the years, but he never takes any of them out more than once or twice."

"Juliet, if your mom was anything like you, he'll probably never be able to replace her. Before I met you, I had given up on finding a girl I'd want to marry. I had decided that I'd just have to live the life of a lonely bachelor."

Juliet met Michael's parents, Steve and Leah Nelson, for the first time at the rehearsal dinner the night before the wedding. They lived in New York, where Steve was an insurance executive, and had just arrived that day. Kind and gracious, they were clearly proud of their only child and seemed pleased to see him so happy with Juliet. Michael's mom, a real theater buff, sat next to Leonard at the rehearsal dinner and talked to him about Shakespeare most of the evening.

As the dinner group broke up later that evening, Juliet was frustrated to still have so little information on how to pack for the honeymoon. Michael was in charge of making the plans and, as usual, was keeping them a big secret. All he would tell her was that she should bring things suitable for the tropics.

Early on the morning of the wedding, Leah Nelson picked Juliet up for breakfast at Mollies Country Cafe. Leah had told Juliet at the rehearsal dinner that she was sorry to have missed all the excitement of planning for the wedding and wanted a chance to get to know her future daughter-in-law. After they ordered their breakfast, Leah smiled gently and said, "Michael told me that your mother died when you were in high school."

"Yes. I've been really missing her these past few months. This is a time in my life that I so wanted her to share with me. She was such a romantic—the love of my dad's life. I wish she had been able to meet Michael and see how perfect he is for me. She would have been so happy."

"I think she must be watching you from heaven and smiling her blessings down on you. You know, I've always regretted not having a daughter, Juliet. I'm so pleased that you'll be a member of our family now. I was beginning to think that my picky son would never find a girl perfect enough for his tastes. I'm glad he found you."

Juliet stirred some cream into her coffee and said, "Michael always gives me a goofy answer when I ask him about it, but I've often wondered how such a handsome, wonderful guy hasn't had some girl catch him at the altar before now."

"Ever since Michael was in high school, he's had the same all-consuming obsession his father has—the passion to make a success of himself. Michael's dad is a self-confessed workaholic, and I think our boy has a lot of that in him, too."

"Why do you suppose he's like that?"

"In the early years of our marriage and when Michael was a little boy, we really struggled financially. Steve was getting his business degree at night school and working full-time, and I'm afraid Michael picked up on our desperation to get ahead at all costs."

"Don't feel bad that you went through some hard times, Mrs. Nelson. I think it's probably given Michael a lot of his character and drive."

"Please, call me Leah. Or I'd love to have you call me Mom, if you're comfortable with that."

Juliet's eyes filled with tears. As she looked across the table at the attractive, petite woman with the warm smile, she realized that marrying Michael was going to be more of a blessing than she had expected. "I've been waiting for six years to have someone to call 'Mom' again. I never realized how blessed I'd become when I met your son."

"Dear, what I'm trying to tell you is that something in you has inspired my son to think about more in life than the health of his savings account. I think you're going to help him become a happier, more well-rounded person. But I have to warn you that I see the same disease in Michael that I struggle with in his father. Both of them just don't know when to leave the office and take a break."

"What do you do about it?"

"I'm not all that assertive, but when Steve has too many weeks of late nights, I simply insist that we go away for a weekend. We have an old cabin that I bought years ago with an inheritance I received when my mother died. I really got it for Steve. He enjoys tinkering around the place. And it doesn't have a phone!"

"So Michael never even got close to marriage in thirty years?"

"Well, one girl I remember soon after he graduated from the university seemed determined to pin him down. One thing I've noticed about Michael, though, is that he's old-fashioned enough to want to do the chasing. I don't think he liked her persistence, and finally she gave up in disgust."

Leah asked their waitress to bring the check and then pulled out a small, red velvet jewelry box and handed it to Juliet. "Over thirty-three years ago, when I was about to marry Steve, my mother gave me this necklace. It's been a tradition in my family since my grandmother's wedding for the mother to give this necklace to her oldest daughter. I consider you to be my daughter now."

Juliet opened the box and gasped in delight. From a delicate chain hung a gold-rimmed oval cameo depicting three ladies in long, flowing dresses, holding hands and dancing in a circle. She studied its incredibly minute detail.

"I've never seen anything like this in my entire life. It's so lovely! Thank you, Mom. This will go beautifully with my wedding dress. It can be my 'something old.' I was going to fudge a little and consider my underwear the 'something old' part."

"According to our family history, my great-grandmother went to the coast of Italy for her honeymoon and my great-grandfather bought this for her as a souvenir."

"Speaking of honeymoons, has your son told you where he's taking me on our honeymoon? I am so worried that I haven't packed the right clothes."

"He has, but I've been sworn to secrecy. If you don't have the right clothes, make him take you shopping for some new ones. That's what he deserves for keeping you in the dark."

"I'm relieved to hear you say that we'll be at a place where we can shop. All Michael has told me is to bring things that I can wear in the tropics. I feel as though I'm leaving for the jungle with Tarzan right after the wedding."

Leah laughed. "Oh, Juliet, I can see why Michael couldn't resist you. I'm so glad you're going to be my daughter."

By the time they walked out to Leah's rental car, Juliet felt as though she had a new friend and ally. In fact, Leah made Juliet promise that if she ran into any confusing territory, she'd give her new mom a call.

Later that morning, Jessica took the bride-to-be to her favorite beauty salon in Scott's Valley. She was going to treat herself and her younger sister to "the works"—a facial, leg waxing, manicure, pedicure, shampoo, and styling. Jessica was every bit as pretty as her sister, but her medium-brown, shoulder-length hair and hazel eyes didn't create the striking impression that Juliet's black hair and blue eyes did.

The beautician and manicurist became very enthusiastic when they realized they were getting Juliet and Jessica ready for a wedding. Juliet felt as if she were a little girl again, playing "beauty salon" with her sister. They had a wonderful time being pampered and made to look totally gorgeous.

Dan had taken Leonard to pick up his tuxedo, so the house was empty when the girls returned to Jessica's that afternoon. The two sisters sat at the kitchen table, drinking tea and eating peanut butter toast. Jessica seemed flustered and finally blurted out, "I feel like I need to give you some advice or something. I know that moms usually talk to their daughters about what to expect on the wedding night, and I'm trying to think what Mom would have told you."

"So that's why you've been acting so weird. Don't worry about me, Jessie. I've taken many health classes in all my years of school. I think I know what to expect."

"I just want to tell you how proud I am of you for saving yourself for your husband. I know Mom would have been proud of you, too. I remember being engaged to Dan. It isn't easy to wait."

"The amazing thing is, Jessie, Mom did talk to me about falling in love someday with the man I would marry. She told me that she was a virgin when she married Dad. She thought that was one of the reasons their marriage was so special. I always thought they had the greatest marriage, and I've reminded myself of Mom's advice when I've gotten too tempted with Michael."

"I remember when she was helping me pack to leave for my freshman year at Davis. She said, 'Why should a man buy a cow when he can get the milk for free?'"

Juliet burst out laughing. "Oh, Jess, remember this one? 'Anything worth having is worth waiting for.' Mom was full of great sayings. Wouldn't she be happy to think we've remembered some of them?"

Jessica lifted her teacup to her sister for a toast. "Here's to my darling little sister, Juliet. May you and Michael have the second greatest marriage of all time." In the next breath, Jessica announced that Juliet should take a nap, no arguing allowed.

"Oh, right, Jessie! I'm about to marry Prince Charming, and you really think I'll be able to lie down and fall asleep. Besides, my hair may get messed up."

"We can touch up your hair, but you've got a big night ahead of you and you'll be glad if you have your wits about you. At least you can lie down and close your eyes. Believe me, you'll be much more beautiful if you do."

The appeal to her vanity did the trick, and Juliet was shocked when her travel alarm went off and she saw that she'd slept for over an hour. As she lay on the bed in Jessica's guest room, she realized that the next time she went to bed, she'd be with her new husband. The idea made her feel more excited than nervous. She'd been longing for this night to come.

Early in their engagement, Michael had confessed to Juliet that he had been physically intimate with a few women in the past. He told her how sorry he was that Juliet wouldn't be the only lover he'd ever had. He said that Juliet was everything he'd always dreamed of, but over the years, he had just about lost hope of ever finding her.

She knew that she could trust Michael to be understanding and patient with her inexperience. She was so impressed with his gentlemanly behavior and the respect he had for her desire to conduct their engagement God's way. There had been times during the past few weeks when she had wanted to give in to temptation and spend the night with him in their new house, but he had always talked her out of it. He insisted that he wanted their first night in their new bedroom to be as husband and wife. She loved him all the more for that.

Chapter Four

Leonard and Juliet arrived at the Mount Hermon chapel that evening around six o'clock. Jessica and Dan had been there for over an hour, handling the many pre-wedding details. Jessica was lighting candles up on the platform at the front of the chapel when Juliet walked in. She rushed over to her younger sister and exclaimed, "Look at you! All that shopping we did was worth every minute. You are glowing."

Juliet wore a long, white, satin and lace gown. The unique tan-and-white cameo necklace was a perfect length for the scoop of the neckline on her wedding dress. She had pulled the sides of her hair to the back of her head with a barrette, to which she had fastened lilies of the valley. The effect was simple and elegant.

Juliet felt as if she were walking in her sleep as she glided to the front of the chapel to look at the gorgeous arrangements of pink and white roses and lilies of the valley. "The florist did an incredible job; this is just the way I dreamed it would look," she said in a voice that sounded far away to her own ears.

Jessica looked prettier than ever, too, in a long, dark blue, velvet gown. She studied her younger sister with concern. "Julie, are you okay? You seem almost too calm."

"This moment is hard to explain, Jessie. I've fantasized about this day ever since I was a little girl, daydreaming my way through long church sermons. Now that I'm here, I almost feel like I'm having an out-of-body experience. Is this really happening?"

"Yes, this is all real. And we need to go to the dressing room right now. Michael will be here any minute, and I don't want him to get even a peek at you before you walk up the aisle."

While they were waiting in the bride's little dressing room, Leonard stepped in to check on his daughters. "Girls, the chapel is filling up, and I think we'll be ready to start any minute. Before you go out there and become Michael's bride, Juliet, I want to tell you how much I love you. You are going to be a wonderful wife for him, just the way you've been a devoted helper to me all these years. I can't even begin to tell you girls how proud I am of both of you." His chin started to quiver as he hugged each of his daughters. "Hey, now don't start to cry, girls. You've got to look good for the photographer!"

"Well, I have to say, Dad, that if you wore a tux to the college every day, we'd have a new stepmother in a month or two. You look so handsome." Jessica straightened the sprig of lily of the valley on his lapel. His thick white hair made a striking contrast to the black tuxedo.

A few minutes later as Juliet looked up the aisle at Michael, standing next to his best man, Bill, she saw that he was clearly overwhelmed. His eyes hardly left her during the wedding ceremony, and after the minister had pronounced them husband and wife, Michael whispered something to Bill and whisked Juliet outside to the waiting limousine. As they drove away from the chapel, Juliet turned to Michael with dismay. "Honey, weren't we supposed to stand in a receiving line at the back of the chapel?"

"Juliet, I know that's what we planned at the rehearsal last night, but I couldn't wait another minute to be alone with you. You look so incredible, and I had to kiss you more than would have been appropriate for the end of the ceremony."

They kissed and cuddled until they were almost at Chaminade, and then Juliet asked, "Do you think our guests know what they're supposed to do?"

"I told Bill before we left to send everyone over here. If we're lucky, we'll have five, maybe ten minutes before the crowd arrives." As they walked through the lobby of Chaminade, Michael pointed out the pretty view of Santa Cruz, lit up in the valley below them.

"Even a moonlit panoramic view of the city doesn't compare with the way you look tonight, Michael. Do you have any idea how handsome you are in that tuxedo?"

"I've been thinking the same thoughts about you, sweetheart. You just seem to grow lovelier by the minute."

As they walked into the ballroom, Juliet let out a little gasp of delight. She and Jessica had arranged for twenty potted trees to be rented for the evening and decorated with tiny white lights. Small white candles and lilies of the valley graced every table. The effect was even more enchanting than she had anticipated. The ballroom had been transformed into a starlit garden party.

As Michael had predicted, the guests soon began arriving, and he proudly introduced them to his new bride. Michael had made many friends over the years selling real estate, and they were all eager to meet the girl who had finally convinced him to settle down. As they dined on delicious seafood Newburg and prime rib and danced to romantic songs from the 1940s, '50s, and '60s, Juliet was able to relax and enjoy the beautiful evening that all her hours of planning had helped to create.

Finally, the cake had been cut, the garter and bride's bouquet had been tossed, and it was time to leave for their honeymoon. Juliet had been talking to a childhood friend who had caught the bouquet when she realized that Michael was nowhere in sight. She walked around the ballroom, saying good-bye to their family and friends and looking for Michael, and finally found him talking intently to Bill. She came up behind him and whispered, "Can we please go on our honeymoon now?"

He grabbed Juliet's hand and practically ran out of the ballroom with her in a shower of rice the guests tossed at their backs. As they walked through the lobby, Juliet asked Michael where he had gone after she tossed her bouquet. He explained that Bill had been helping him take their luggage to a hotel room. Juliet was surprised to discover that they were staying at Chaminade for the night and asked Michael if they were going to stay in Santa Cruz for their whole honeymoon.

"Sweetheart, I just didn't think you'd feel like flying anywhere tonight. I'll tell you where we're going on the way to the airport tomorrow afternoon. I promise." They walked along the lighted outdoor pathway to their room and Michael unlocked the door and carried Juliet across the threshold. He stood her down near the doorway and watched her take in the scene.

Glowing white candles, in many different sizes, had been placed on every available surface in the room. Through the open door to the bathroom, she could see that candles were lit on the sink top, as well. And on the bed, spread across the turned-down covers, were about two-dozen, pink, long-stemmed roses. The realization of how much her new husband must cherish her to go to so much trouble boggled her mind. Suddenly the calm and cool exterior she had shown during the entire wedding and reception melted away in a flood of tears.

"Juliet, what's wrong? Are you disappointed?" Michael sat her down on the side of the bed and took her in his arms. "I know it's not exactly a honeymoon suite–that's why I put all the candles and flowers in the room."

"Oh no, honey, how could I possibly be disappointed

with this? This is more beautiful than anything I could ever have dreamed of. I'm just completely overwhelmed by you, Michael. I can't imagine what I've ever done to deserve such devotion. You're just too good to be true."

"Hmm . . . that sounds like the words to a song we danced to tonight. Sweetheart, what you've done to deserve my devotion is just to be you—Juliet Kendrick Nelson. The girl I've waited thirty years to spend this moment with. Just enjoy it. Let me love you. There's nothing I want to do more."

And he proved it to her all during that long, unforgettable night. Juliet was exhausted, but she didn't want to fall asleep and miss a moment of the night when she became Michael's wife. She finally dozed off in his arms as the sun began turning the sky a lovely rose color. She awoke a few hours later to the smell of coffee and the sight of her gorgeous husband smiling down at her from the side of the bed.

"Good morning, beautiful. Do you want a cup of this? It really hits the spot."

"Thank you, honey."

"How are you feeling? Tired?"

"I don't know how to describe how I'm feeling because I've never felt like this in my entire life. It's as if something became alive in me last night. You've brought out a side to me that never existed before. I think I'm going to love being your wife."

Michael tossed back his head and laughed and fell onto the bed next to his adoring new wife.

Later on the way to the airport, Juliet could not stand the suspense one moment longer. "Michael Nelson, I think I have been more than patient waiting to find out where you're taking me on this mystery honeymoon of ours. What are we going to do if I haven't packed any of the right clothes?"

"We could stay in our room and make-believe we're Adam and Eve. You know, that's actually an excellent idea. You'd make a terrific Eve with that long hair of yours."

"Michael, I'm serious!" But she laughed as she said it. The truth was, she was so crazy in love with this new husband of hers, she wouldn't care if he checked them into a motel in downtown San Jose.

"All right, Juliet. You win. In fact, your reward for being so patient is two, fun-filled weeks on Gilligan's Island!"

"Gilligan's Island! Will you please be serious for one minute? I am dying of curiosity."

"Don't you think Gilligan's Island is a real place? Where do you suppose they filmed the TV show?"

"In a Hollywood studio? Are we going to Los Angeles?"

"Juliet, I'm talking about the *real* Gilligan's Island. I'm taking you to Kauai, to the actual beach where the show was filmed."

"Oh, honey, I was hoping we were going someplace like that. I think I have all the right stuff in my suitcase. You are absolutely the best."

After they settled into their airplane seats for the long flight across the Pacific Ocean, Juliet said, "So tell me more about this honeymoon destination of ours."

"Well, this is the part of the honeymoon where I get to be surprised too," Michael admitted.

"You mean you don't know anything about the place where we're staying?"

"All Joe told me is that it's a one-bedroom cottage with daily maid service on the beach at Hanalei Bay."

"Hanalei Bay—isn't that where they filmed the musical *South Pacific*?"

"Could be. Joe says it's spectacular."

"Who's Joe?"

"He's a guy who used to work with me at Redwood Real Estate. He moved to Kauai a couple of years ago. I trust his taste completely. And because he's a personal friend, I was able to ask him to do things I wouldn't ask a regular broker to do."

"What are you up to now, Michael? You don't have to surprise me anymore. You'll hopelessly spoil me if you don't stop!"

"You've had most of your big surprises. I just gave Joe a grocery list so our cabin would be stocked with food."

By the time they picked up their rental car and found their way to the north end of the island, the sun was starting to set. It looked to Juliet as if this little rustic cottage was the only place for miles around. She turned to Michael and said, "You weren't kidding about playing Adam and Eve, were you? This looks like the Garden of Eden!"

"That's right," he answered, gazing lovingly into her eyes. "And you're my Eve."

As Juliet thought back over those precious days of their honeymoon, she realized that they had enjoyed a magical start to their marriage. Even after they returned to their real lives in Mount Hermon, the honeymoon didn't end. Juliet, who normally hated to get up in the morning, set her alarm clock to go off early so she could have time to enjoy her new husband before she had to go to her first class at UC Santa Cruz. She had transferred there for the spring semester and would be graduating that June. They had truly adored one another, and most of their friends were envious of the obvious passion they had for each other.

She tried to think back to when things first started to cool off between them. It seemed to creep in sometime after Heather was born and Michael's father died unexpectedly of a stroke. Michael went through a real rough time after that, questioning the value of working like a fiend day after day, just to drop over dead at the office before you could retire and enjoy the fruits of your hard work.

Juliet had never suspected Michael of falling in love with another woman; even in their dreariest moments, he always told his friends that she was his dream girl. It just seemed that the issues of life crowded in on them until they began to lose one another.

It was starting to get chilly, and Juliet wanted to have dinner ready before Sally brought the girls home.

Heathcliff was looking at her with questions in his intelligent, dark brown eyes. She rubbed the thick white ruff of fur that made a fluffy collar around his neck and stood out in beautiful contrast against his black-and-white coat. "You know me so well, don't you, Heathcliff? Sometimes I think you know me better than anyone does. Oh, Heathcliff, how am I going to find Daddy again?" The little Border collie may not have understood everything she was saying to him, but the unconditional love and loyalty she saw in his eyes was a balm for her heart. She gathered up her picnic things and walked back to the house with Heathcliff on her heels.

Michael drove his car into the driveway as she was coming up the sidewalk. He rolled down his window and asked, "Did you go for a hike?"

"Yes, it was so pretty in the woods today. Sorry you missed it. How was your day?"

"I think the Andersons have found their house. Listen, I'm sorry I had to work this weekend. Maybe next time you want to have some time alone with me, you could let me know in advance, and I'll try to free up my schedule."

"Yeah, I'm a slow learner, but I'm starting to realize that surprises don't work for a real estate agent."

Chapter Five

Juliet was dumping spaghetti into a colander when Sally came into the kitchen with the girls. It would be good to have their noise and commotion in the house again. Maybe that was the answer for Juliet's depression, to keep busy and surrounded with activity.

It was such a blessing to have a best friend with kids the same age right up the street. Juliet teasingly referred to Sally as her "California girlfriend." She was the epitome of the California girl, with her sun-streaked blond hair, tan skin, beautiful white smile, and athletic figure. She was also the kind of friend you could call any time of the day or night.

The two women had met shortly after Michael and Juliet's wedding, when they all went to a neighborhood dinner sponsored by their church. The people from Seaside Bible Church who lived in the Felton and Mount Hermon areas met once a month for a potluck dinner and a chance to get to know other Christians in their neighborhood. Sally and Juliet had so much to talk about from that first evening, and now Juliet felt that, besides Michael and Jessica, no one was closer to her than Sally.

When Daisy Marie had been born eight years ago, Sally was the first friend to come and hold her. And when Sally and John had Katie a year later, Juliet was thrilled and hoped that the little girls would become best friends, just like their moms. The girls' friendship was inevitable, as the two mothers had a standing invitation to drop by each other's homes at any time to get a break from a colicky baby or just to share some coffee and adult conversation.

Now, with Heather six years old and in school all day, Juliet was away from home more often, teaching Dancercise classes three days a week and volunteering at the school. Next year, Sally would have more free time as well because her little boy, Johnny, would be old enough for kindergarten.

"How are my little darlings? I missed you girls!" Juliet knelt down in front of the kitchen sink and hugged and kissed her daughters, then she smiled up at her friend. "How did it go, Sally?"

"We had a wonderful time, and I assure you that everyone will sleep well tonight. I could still hear the girls talking in Katie's room around midnight, but I was too tired to tell them to go to sleep."

"Do you have time to have a cup of coffee with me?"

"No, John's cooking some hamburgers on the grill, and I've got to get back. What did you and Michael decide about the marriage enrichment weekend? I have to have my final count after church tomorrow morning so I can turn in all the reservations and deposits."

"Michael hasn't said yes or no yet; he's positively phobic about making any plans on the weekends. Says it's his best time to show houses."

"Well, try to talk him into it. He'll have a great time once you get there."

"Okay. I'll try my best. Thanks for keeping the girls for me. Your turn is next, remember."

"Yeah, I know. John is talking about going camping near Carmel before it gets too cold."

"That should be fun. Just tell me when."

"Okay. Bye. See you at church in the morning."

Dinner was ready, and Juliet went looking for Michael and the girls. She found them out on the deck, tossing a baseball back and forth. Michael was determined that his girls would be the best kids on the Little League team next spring, regardless of their gender.

After dinner, while the girls were playing in the bath, Juliet sat down next to Michael in his recliner and brought up the subject of the marriage enrichment weekend.

"Didn't we just have a couple's weekend?"

"Michael, you aren't seriously going to call this past weekend a couple's weekend, are you?"

"You have a point. When is it again?"

"The third weekend in October. You'll have enough time to plan your appointments around it."

"What about Daisy and Heather?"

"They can stay with my sister. She's even agreed to take Heathcliff. I've already asked her."

"It sounds like you've got everything covered, but I'm just not very excited at the thought of paying money to sit through a bunch of lectures all weekend."

"I know you're not excited about going, Michael. But you should know how desperate I am to see some positive changes in this marriage of ours. We're sinking."

"You're still the most dramatic girl I know."

"Can I tell Sally yes tomorrow?"

"Go ahead." He picked up the remote control for the television and began to click through the channels.

Juliet went upstairs to take the girls out of their bath. Heather was practically asleep before Juliet could dry her off, put on her pajamas, and tuck her into bed, but Daisy was a night owl like her mom. Even after her tiring sleep over at Sally's, Daisy was anxious to talk to Juliet about her day at school on Friday.

"We had a substitute teacher yesterday, and she's going to have a baby."

"Really! How wonderful! Where was Mrs. Johnson?"

"She had to fly to New Hampshire to be in her sister's wedding. The substitute teacher told us right away that she was going to have a baby at Christmas time. She didn't want us to think she was just fat."

Juliet laughed at her daughter's blunt way of putting things. "Having a baby is the most beautiful miracle in a person's life."

"Mommy, tell me again about when I got born."

"Again? Daisy, I feel like I tell you this story three times a week." She pulled the covers down on Daisy's bed and tucked her in.

"Pleeease," she whined. "Then I'll go right to sleep, I promise."

"Well my stomach started really hurting and I told Daddy—"

"No, no, no! I want to hear the whole story. Right from when you found out I was in your tummy."

"Okay, but you'll have to make some room for me on your bed. I think I'm more tired than you are." She crawled under the pink flowered quilt next to her daughter and smelled the sweet baby shampoo in the girl's freshly washed hair. Physically, Daisy was a miniature of her mom, with dark hair and blue eyes, but she was assertive and determined like her dad. Heather had blond hair and hazel eyes like Michael and was a sensitive, tenderhearted little peacemaker.

"I'd better turn off the light, so that Heather can sleep better." The girls shared an adorable bedroom decorated in pink flower prints and white wicker. Juliet reached over to turn off the lamp on the nightstand between their two double beds. The room took on a rosy glow from a little flowered nightlight next to the dresser. Then she settled back down next to Daisy with a long sigh.

"Okay, Mommy, you promised."

"Wait, let's call Heathcliff in to lie down with us." Two calls brought the dog bounding into the room and leaping up on the foot of the bed. Juliet reached down to rub his ears as he snuggled against their legs. "I love this dog,

Daisy. All my life I wanted a dog, but we couldn't have one where we lived when I was a little girl. Do you remember when he was just a puppy and wasn't potty trained yet, and we had to make him stay in the kitchen all the time so he wouldn't mess up the house? He would start to howl and bark at bedtime because he was lonely, so I would let you and Heather sleep with him on the kitchen floor in your sleeping bags. Remember that? He was such a cute puppy."

"Mommy, I want to hear about when I was a baby."

"First, your bedtime prayers and then the story." But before Juliet could finish saying Daisy's prayers with her, she could hear her daughter snoring softly. She lay there admiring her sweet little profile and remembering how this precious child had come into their lives.

Juliet and Michael had been married a little over two years. After Juliet graduated from college, she'd taken a job as a physical education teacher at a high school in Santa Cruz. She started a water ballet club that met after school three days a week. One hot afternoon in May, the swimmers were working on the spring water ballet show that they would be performing for their parents the following week. Juliet was walking around the edge of the pool, telling the girls how to keep their lines straighter, when suddenly she crumpled to the deck in a dead faint.

Two girls ran and got the soccer coach, who helped Juliet walk over to the PE office. He made her lie down on the sofa and insisted on calling Michael at work. Michael must have taken the road down to Santa Cruz at a breakneck speed, because he seemed to arrive at the PE office within minutes. Juliet was still feeling dizzy and nauseated and was lying on the sofa with a cold cloth on her forehead, but she sat up when Michael came in.

"Sweetheart, what's going on? What do you think happened?"

"I don't know, honey. I was talking to the girls, and the next thing I knew I was lying on the deck. I was busy doing paperwork and skipped lunch today. Maybe that's why I got so dizzy."

"Juliet, you've skipped lunch plenty of times since I've known you. Have you ever fainted before?"

"No."

"Come on, sweetie. Get your stuff. We're going to the doctor."

"Michael, that's silly. I'm sure I'll be fine. Let's just go home."

"Forget it. You can't talk me out of this." When his voice got that determined sound to it, Juliet knew it was useless to argue, so she asked the soccer coach to send her water ballet team home, and she followed Michael out to his car. An hour later, they left the urgent care center with dazed looks on their faces and a list of recommended obstetricians.

"Michael, I just don't understand it. We were using birth control."

"Well, it obviously didn't work." He grinned at her. "Juliet, I'm so surprised and excited about this, I can hardly think straight."

"You're not upset about the timing? Did you want to have children this soon?"

"Sweetheart, this is incredible. The timing is always right for a miracle. Just think, we're going to have a baby. Our very own baby!" He was practically shouting. "I can't wait to tell our folks."

Those next eight months always stood out in Juliet's mind as one of the dearest times in her life. Michael behaved as if they were the only couple in the world who had ever had a baby. Practically every other day he'd come home from work with another book about childbirth or parenting. Or he would bring something home that he thought the baby would really need, like a new baseball mitt. He fussed over Juliet and acted as if she had a terminal illness.

The only downside to the whole experience was that Michael became concerned about being intimate with her once she started showing. Juliet tried repeatedly to tell him that they didn't need to stop being together just because she was getting bigger. "Michael, you've read more books about pregnancy than I have. Every one of them says you can make love the whole nine months if everything is going well."

"I would just never forgive myself if something happened to the poor little guy."

Finally, Juliet stopped pestering him about it and figured it was only a few more months. It was a happy, busy time for them, as they turned their extra bedroom into a nursery and took natural childbirth classes at the hospital one night each week.

Juliet hadn't gone back to teaching that fall. Michael wouldn't hear of it. He insisted that he made more than enough money to support them all and that their baby deserved to have a full-time mom. Juliet didn't argue with him. She had always loved having her mom at home while she was growing up. Besides, she was planning to breast-feed and that seemed almost impossible to pull off with a job outside the home.

Once she got used to the idea of being a full-time home-maker, she found that she really loved it. For a change, she had the time and energy to make special dinners for Michael, knit little sweaters for the baby, and take up counted cross-stitching again. They had decided not to let the doctor tell them the sex of their baby before it was born. This added to their suspense as the delivery day approached.

They celebrated their third anniversary quietly that year. Juliet was feeling like a beached whale and spent most of her waking hours on the sofa, cross-stitching a sampler for the baby. It was impossible to find a comfortable position to sleep in at night, and everything she ate gave her indigestion. Michael came in from work on the night of their anniversary with a bouquet of pink roses and told her they had a dinner reservation at the Sunset Dining Room at Chaminade. "We can go back to the place where it all started. Sweetheart, why are you crying?"

"Oh, Michael, how can you even stand to take me out in public. Look at me!"

"I am looking at you, Juliet. You're the most attractive

woman I've ever known. The fact that you're carrying our child makes you even more beautiful in my eyes. Come on, I'll help you put on that pretty blue satin dress, and we'll go out for some seafood. You'll feel better when you get a change of scenery."

It did lift her spirits to sit in the elegant restaurant overlooking the city and remember their wedding reception three years before. When they considered how much their lives had changed in that short amount of time, Juliet and Michael were amazed.

Two weeks later, Juliet woke up Michael before his alarm went off. She'd been feeling more miserable than usual all night but wondered if the pains she was having were just a false alarm. Dr. Greer, their obstetrician, had told them that most first-time parents make the mistake of rushing to the hospital at the first little twinge and either have to be sent back home or spend hours in labor at the hospital.

She remembered that their childbirth instructor had told the moms-to-be to soak in the bathtub when they had contractions and that if the pains stopped, it was probably just a false alarm. But after soaking for a little more than an hour, Juliet's contractions had become stronger and picked up speed. Now it was time to let Michael in on the situation. She came out of the bathroom wearing her favorite old, blue, terry cloth robe and looked down at her sleeping husband.

She placed her hand on his arm and tried to keep her voice calm. "Honey, I've been having contractions all night long. I timed them for the past hour, and they seem to be following a pattern."

"What!" She had never seen him wake up so quickly. "How often are you having them?"

"Every three minutes."

"What! But Dr. Greer told us to call him when they were every five minutes." He pulled on his pants and dug around in the closet for his shoes.

"Well, I didn't really take them all that seriously till the last hour or so, but now . . ." She started to moan as a hideous pain ripped through her stomach, and she ran to the bathroom to throw up.

Michael yelled through the bathroom door that she should get dressed while he called the doctor and then let his real estate office know that he wouldn't be coming in to work. Juliet felt too miserable to do anything but crawl back into bed. She was lying on her side and breathing deeply, as she had been taught to do in the childbirth classes, when he came back from making his phone calls.

"Sweetheart, it's time to go."

"Oh, Michael, I don't want to go anywhere. Please don't make me get up."

"Juliet, come on. We've got to get you dressed and out to the car." He helped her pull on the gray turtleneck shirt and denim jumper she had taken off the night before. He grabbed the suitcase they'd had packed and waiting at the garage door for the past two weeks.

The drive to the hospital was agonizing for Juliet. She could not get comfortable sitting in the front seat with a seat belt on. She wanted to stretch out on her side, but Michael didn't want to stop the car and let her get into the back seat. A few times the contractions were so strong that she could not keep from screaming. The pain was so disorienting, Juliet didn't even recognize the familiar streets of Santa Cruz.

"Michael, Michael, are we almost there?" she wailed as he gripped the steering wheel and stared at the car crawling ahead of them in the morning rush-hour traffic.

"Sweetheart, look, we just crossed Morrissey Boulevard; we'll be there any minute. Hold on. Just keep taking great big breaths."

Finally they arrived at the hospital, where staff assisted Juliet into a wheelchair and took her immediately to a birthing room. Dr. Greer was already in the room, scrubbing up. He checked Juliet, who was in tears, and told her that it would be time to push after a couple more contractions.

"Can you give her something for the pain, Dr. Greer?" Juliet was glad to hear Michael asking for painkillers. They had planned to have the baby with no medications, but she was beyond trying to be heroic.

"This baby is going to be born so soon that the painkiller wouldn't have time to kick in. Don't worry, Mike, she's doing great."

Michael hurried to scrub his hands and put on a hospital gown, but before he finished, the nurse began urging Juliet to push. She was crying and trembling uncontrollably and saying that she couldn't. Michael sat down next to her and held her hands. "Juliet, Julie honey, listen. Our baby is almost here. You have to push. Here, I'll do it with you. Open your eyes. Look into my eyes, sweetheart." Dr. Greer looked at the fetal monitor and nodded to Michael that it was time to push again. "Okay, sweetheart, this is it. Big breath and hold it. Push! One, two, three, four, five . . ." He didn't make it to six because Juliet let out a scream that seemed to rise up from the soles of her feet. Then a high, thin baby's wail filled the room.

As the doctor lifted up a very wet and wrinkled baby girl and laid her on Juliet's stomach, Juliet and Michael both cried. The doctor cut the umbilical cord, and a nurse wrapped Daisy in a pink blanket and placed her in Michael's arms. "Juliet, look. We have a tiny girl. And she is exquisite, just like her mommy." He tucked Daisy on the bed next to Juliet. The new parents couldn't take their eyes off their tiny baby.

Dr. Greer delivered the afterbirth, and the nurse cleaned off Juliet and covered her with some fresh, heated blankets, but Juliet was hardly aware of any of the activity in the room. All she could do was gaze into the serious blue eyes of her precious little girl and marvel at the whole experience. She knew she would never forget these moments as long as she lived.

After the nurse had helped Juliet figure out the first breast-feeding and had taken Daisy to the nursery for an examination and a fresh baby blanket, she came back with the adorable little bundle and laid her in a bassinet next to Juliet's bed. The nurse told Michael that it was time for his wife and baby to get some sleep, so he left to make some phone calls.

He returned to the hospital three hours later with a bouquet of pink roses and daisies and a birthday cake. After her nap, Juliet had taken a shower and washed her hair and felt positively perky. "Sweetheart, you look gorgeous. How do you feel?"

"Michael, it's amazing. As horrible as I felt this morning, I feel like I could run a marathon now. We did it! I'm so relieved it's all over. Honey, thank you for being so strong for me at the end there. I don't know how I could have gotten through it all without you."

"I wouldn't have missed it for anything. I am so proud of you, Juliet. I've never had an experience like that before. I was terrified on the way to the hospital that I would have to pull over on the side of the road and deliver the baby myself."

She giggled, "I thought I heard you offering a prayer of thanks when we pulled into the parking lot. Next time, I won't wait so long to leave for the hospital."

He studied their baby girl, sleeping peacefully next to her mom. He lifted her tiny hand and said, "I felt like I was watching a miracle take place right in front of my eyes. I'll never forget it. So when can we have another one?"

Heather Leah, their next little miracle, came almost exactly two years after her big sister's arrival. By then, Michael and Juliet felt like seasoned veterans and had the endless diaper changes and middle-of-the-night breast-feeding sessions all figured out. Of course, having two adorable but demanding little daughters in the house brought any remnants of a honeymoon to a screeching halt.

One of the things Michael used to love was for Juliet to take a shower with him before they went to bed at night. One evening, as they were turning off the lights in the living room and heading upstairs for bed, Michael asked her to join him in the shower. Juliet smiled at him and said she'd take their empty ice-cream bowls out to the kitchen and be right up.

But as she passed the girls' room on her way down the hall, she heard Heather crying. She knew that if she didn't go in right away and nurse Heather back to sleep, Daisy would soon be awake, too. As she sat in the girls' darkened room and rocked and nursed her baby, she could hear the shower running and running. She felt horrible to think of Michael in there, waiting for her, but she didn't want to break the spell of lulling Heather back to dreamland. When she finally put the sleeping baby back in her crib and found Michael in their bedroom, he seemed annoyed. "Where'd you go?"

"Honey, I'm so sorry I didn't make it in time. Heather was waking up, and I had to nurse her back to sleep."

"I waited and waited until the water was actually cold."

"I'm really sorry. Maybe next time."

"Yeah. Whatever." But he never gave her a chance to make it up to him. She even suggested several times in later weeks and months that they get in the shower together, but he never wanted to. It broke her heart and made her feel frustrated because it seemed as if he held it against her for being a mom when he wanted her to be a lover. It was a no-win situation in her mind, and Juliet felt torn in half. She had tried to talk to him about it a few times and apologize, but he always acted like it was no big deal.

In spite of the changes it made in their lifestyle, Michael said he loved having babies and would be happy to add a new one to their nest every two years, but he didn't pressure Juliet about it. He said he knew that she paid a much bigger price for every new member they added to their family, so he told her the decision of when and if they'd have another baby was up to her.

Juliet looked over at six-year-old Heather, asleep in her bed, and wondered if it was too late to go back to the new-baby phase again. She was so pleased with their two little girls and was really enjoying the freedom she had in her life again, now that they were both in school. She was only thirty-three years old and could easily try for the little boy she knew Michael would love to have. She just didn't know if she was ready to go back to being so tied down and exhausted from having her sleep disturbed every night. She slipped out from under the covers on Daisy's bed and walked down the hallway to her bedroom.

Juliet knelt down next to the white love seat to stroke Sheba, who was settled into her sleeping spot in front of the fireplace and purring loudly. Juliet kissed her on her soft white forehead, as the cat cracked open one blue eye to gaze at her admirer. "I wish I could be like you, Sheba, so content and mellow," she whispered in her little friend's ear. The cat watched benevolently from her cozy spot as Juliet changed out of her jeans and into her old flannel nightgown.

Michael was sound asleep and didn't move when she got into bed next to him. Many nights she had fallen asleep in the girls' beds after she had told them their bedtime stories, and Michael didn't seem to notice or miss her. She wondered how many husbands and wives fell asleep at night feeling as if they were lying in bed next to a stranger.

Chapter Six

Three weeks later, on a Friday afternoon, Juliet picked the girls up after school and drove them and Heathcliff over to her sister's house in Scott's Valley. In the years since the wedding, Jessica and Dan had been blessed with a few kids of their own. Their son, Danny, was ten; then they had a little girl, Rachel, who was seven. Kevin was the youngest and had just celebrated his third birthday. Jessica had stopped teaching full time when Danny was born, but she worked occasionally as a substitute.

Daisy and Heather were excited about spending the weekend with their cousins and ran up the stairs to find Rachel in her bedroom. Danny ran out to the backyard with Heathcliff to throw a tennis ball to him. Jessica turned to her sister in mock irritation and complained, "I hope you realize all the trouble you've caused in this family because of that dog of yours. All Danny ever talks about these days is how we need to get a dog like Aunt Julie's."

"You wouldn't regret getting a puppy for the kids. I think every family should have a dog. But to tell you the truth, I'm much crazier about Heathcliff than the girls are. I'd be lost without him. He's the dearest friend in the whole world to me."

"What are you doing with Sheba this weekend?"

"I'm just leaving a bunch of food and water out for her. She's an indoor cat and is so independent that I don't imagine she'll even miss us much for just two days."

Jessica talked Juliet into staying for a cup of tea, and they sat at the kitchen table to eat some of the oatmeal cookies she had just taken from the oven.

"So tell me about this marriage enrichment weekend. What's it all about?"

"Sally was in charge of signing people up for it at our church. She and John have gone a few times, and they say it's really good for their marriage. Helps them to stay focused on the things that make a relationship healthy. We're supposed to sign in before seven o'clock tonight, and we'll listen to a lecture. The rest of the weekend is going to be lectures alternating with questions and exercises you work on with your husband." Juliet reached for the sugar bowl and stirred a spoonful into her tea. "By the way, they have the last session on Sunday after lunch, so we'll probably be back for the girls around five o'clock or so. I'm practically dragging Michael to this. I think he'd be happier putting new stain on our back deck this weekend."

"Why are you going then?"

"Oh, Jessie, we seem to have stalled in a ditch in our marriage, and I'm hoping this will help pull us out."

"You're kidding." Jessica wrinkled her nose and squinted her eyes at her sister. "You and Michael have always been the most passionate couple I've ever known, next to Mom and Dad of course."

"I can see that you think I'm exaggerating, but it's true. Michael's always been wonderful about maintaining a great public image. But when we're alone, it's another story. Sometimes I wonder if he even enjoys having a wife."

"Now I know that's an exaggeration. I've never seen any man more taken with his wife than Michael is with you. I think it's normal for all marriages to settle down after a few years. You can't be on a honeymoon forever. You'd die from exhaustion."

"This is more than just settling down, Jessie. I'm worried about us."

"Maybe having some time away from your normal routine will help you both. What did Michael say about our plans to spend Thanksgiving at Lake Tahoe?"

"He agreed to it after I told him he owed us a vacation. The girls hardly ever spend time with him. We haven't done anything special as a family for so long."

"Julie, I've been meaning to ask you something. Some ladies in our church are starting a new Bible study after everyone has recovered from Christmas. We're going to learn how to become better lovers of God and each other. How about signing up with me? It would be fun to go together, and it sounds like the perfect class for you right now."

"Jessie, I've read so much about love in the past few years, I could probably teach the class. I'm so frustrated with the whole subject of men and women and marriage, if I didn't have two girls to raise, I think I'd consider joining a convent."

"Wow. You are discouraged. I hope this weekend does something to boost your morale."

"I don't mean to be such a downer, Jess. Ask me about the class again after Christmas. Maybe things will be better by then."

Michael got a phone call just as he was leaving his office, so he was late picking up Juliet at their house. They bought sandwiches to eat on the way to the Santa Clara Marriott and showed up half an hour late for the opening lecture. After the first session, they met up with Sally and John for pie and coffee at the Marriott's coffee shop.

"Have you been to your room yet?" Sally asked after the waitress had taken their order. "I'm really pleased that they were able to book the conference at this hotel. Our room is gorgeous. I think I'm going to feel very spoiled this weekend."

"How about you, John? Are you glad to be here, too, or did your wife have to talk you into it like mine did?" Michael asked his friend.

"Give it a chance, Michael. This will be our third conference. I think it's good for us to go to one of these every few years."

"Three times! Don't you get tired of hearing the same lectures?" Michael seemed skeptical.

"They don't have the same speakers every year, even though the topics are always about marriage and family. It's been different every time we've come. Sometimes the best part is just being able to have uninterrupted conversations with Sally." John smiled at his wife, and she reached across the table to hold his hand.

Michael still didn't seem sold on the idea, and Juliet wondered if she had made another bad move when she had insisted they come. Later when they checked into their room, Michael was tired and distracted and just wanted to watch the news and go to sleep. Juliet mustered up all her courage and asked, "Michael, do you ever think about how it used to be for us when we were first married? Do you ever miss the passion?"

"I'm still passionate about you, Juliet. Don't you know that?" he answered as he focused on the weather forecast being shown on television.

It didn't seem worth harping on. Michael was either in denial or his definition of passion had changed over the years. She let it go and went into the bathroom to take off her makeup.

The next morning, Juliet sat next to Michael in the conference hall and looked at the program that had been handed to her as she came in the door. The organizers had lined up some interesting lectures for the day. The first session was called "Finding the Keys to Open Your Mate's Heart." When it ended, couples returned to their rooms with questionnaires to work through together for an hour. Juliet looked at the sheet and asked Michael, "What situation discourages you the most in your daily life?" As he began to pour out his confusion to her, she wondered if they'd had a mini-breakthrough.

"Sometimes I wonder if I'm wasting my life, Juliet. I run my tail off day after day to sell houses to people. When I first started in real estate, I was excited about it. There was no question in my mind that it was my ticket to make the most money. Then when my dad died, I realized that all his time had been spent earning money to have a rich, comfortable life. But did he ever have any free time to enjoy the things he worked so hard for? I'm afraid of ending up like him. I'm just not sure I'm in the right place anymore."

"What does that mean?" Juliet wasn't sure she understood him. "Don't you think every job has aspects about it that are unpleasant? You've been so successful in real estate, Michael. What would you do if you left it?"

"Oh, I don't know. I don't know what I think." The wall had come up again, and Juliet wished she hadn't said anything to break his train of thought.

They went back for the next lecture, "How to Keep Traditional Family Values in an Unconventional World," and then it was time for lunch. Juliet was eager to attend the afternoon session. The men would be meeting in one conference room and the women in another to discuss "Myths About Sex and Marriage." She hoped that she would find the answers to the questions on her heart at that session. It would make the whole weekend worth the trouble. After the lecture about sex, the couples would be free for the rest of the evening and were encouraged to order dinner in their rooms and buy some bubble bath and massage oil at the hotel gift shop.

Juliet was one of the first women to arrive at the conference hall after lunch. She wanted to get a seat near the front of the room so she wouldn't miss anything. Sally was supposed to meet her so they could sit together, but she wasn't there yet, so Juliet found a seat and saved the spot next to hers. Doris Perkins, the woman who would be speaking to them, was attractively dressed in a purple business suit and slightly overweight. She looked to be in her sixties and had recently published a book called *Love for the Long Haul.*

About ten minutes into the lecture, Juliet realized the class was not going to address what was happening in her marriage. Doris was warning the wives that they needed to take an interest in sex. She said it was common for most women to lose interest after they'd been married a few years and perhaps had a child or two. But they needed to remember how important sex is to a man and to be willing to be an enthusiastic partner. Then she proceeded to offer suggestions of what wives could do to keep the excitement going in their love lives. Juliet's heart sank as she realized several of the ideas were things that she had already tried unsuccessfully to do with Michael. She felt as if the room were closing in on her. Tears built up in the back of her throat, forming a hard rock. She grabbed her purse and notebook and quietly left the group to escape to the ladies' room.

Once there, she crossed to the last stall and stood inside it with her back against the door. Mercifully, everyone was attending lectures, so she had the privacy of an empty restroom while she cried out her frustration. She had been crying—deep, wrenching sobs from the pit of her stomach—for almost ten minutes when she realized someone else was in the ladies' room with her. She took some big, slow breaths and tried to calm down.

"Juliet, is that you?" Juliet's heart sank. It was Sally. Now she was trapped. When Sally hadn't arrived in the meeting room before Doris Perkins began speaking, Juliet figured that she had gotten tied up at lunch somewhere with John. Now she would have to explain to Sally why she was hiding in the bathroom, crying.

"Juliet?" She had to answer. There would be no way to avoid the inevitable questions.

"Yes."

"Are you okay?"

"Yes, I'll be out in a minute."

Juliet came out of the stall but avoided Sally's eyes. She went over to the sink and splashed cold water on her face.

"Are you sick, Juliet? I saw you rushing out of the lecture hall and got worried."

"No. I just couldn't handle the things Doris Perkins was telling us to do."

"Come on. Let me buy you a cup of coffee downstairs in the coffee shop."

"No, Sally. I'll be fine. Go back or you'll miss the whole

lecture." Juliet soaked some paper towels in the icy cold water and held them up to her swollen eyes.

"How long have we been friends, Juliet? Would you leave me if I were in here crying?"

"No."

"Come on. Touch up your powder, and we'll go."

As they sat at a corner table in the back of the dimly lit coffee shop, Juliet sipped her coffee, looked down at her hands, and sighed.

"What did Doris say that upset you so much?"

Juliet saw the sweet, concerned expression on Sally's face and wondered if God was giving her an opportunity to share her burdens. Sally had proven to be a loyal friend for more than eleven years. Juliet knew that she was not a gossip, and in many ways, she felt closer to Sally than to Jessica. "I don't know what they're teaching the men in their session right now, Sally, but Michael should have been listening to Doris's advice, not me. In our marriage, I'm the one who wants to have a good sex life, and Michael doesn't seem to care." Juliet put her hands over her face, horrified at what she had just blurted out to her friend. "I shouldn't be saying this. It feels so disloyal."

"Juliet, you know I love both you and Michael. I'm not going to share what you're telling me with anyone, not even John."

"I know you won't. I love Michael, too. He is the most wonderful and the kindest man I've ever known. But we're in a terrible place right now. And it's not just our sex life. We don't really talk to each other anymore. At least not about anything that's important. Just a bunch of superficial stuff."

"How long has it been like this?"

"I guess it started sometime after Heather was born and has gotten worse over the years. The thing that upsets me so much is that I've tried most of the ideas Doris was suggesting to recharge your love life, and none of it has ever worked for us. It makes me feel like we're a hopeless case. But the other thing that disturbs me is that I'm not anything like the typical housewife Doris was describing. I've never been disinterested in sex. I wonder what's wrong with me."

Sally giggled, but when she looked at her friend's serious expression, she quickly apologized. "Juliet, I'm sorry. That just seems like such a non-problem. Do you know how many women wish they could muster up a little interest in their sex lives? And how many husbands would love to have a wife with your problem?"

"Well, what good is a strong sex drive to me? I wish I could be like those wives Doris was describing. Then Michael and I would be compatible." Juliet looked around the coffee shop at the nearby tables, which were empty, and lowered her voice to a whisper. "It just makes me feel weird to be so abnormal. Like some kind of sex freak."

Sally started laughing again and apologizing at the same time. "Trust me, Juliet. You're not a freak. Michael is an attractive man. It's normal for you to want to be with him."

"It just seems like some sort of cosmic joke to me. Here I am, apparently one of the only wives on the planet who really enjoys making love with her husband, and I happen to be married to one of the only men who has no interest in it."

"I don't believe that. I don't think God plays 'cosmic jokes' on us. In fact, I don't think anything that happens in a Christian's life is a mistake. God has you and Michael together for a reason."

Juliet buried her face in her hands and rubbed her forehead with her fingertips. Then she looked up at Sally, feeling completely defeated. "I know you're right, Sally. It just doesn't make my life any less frustrating."

"I wonder if Michael isn't the one with the problem. Has he had a physical lately? Maybe his hormones are messed up."

"I wish it was a problem we could solve with a pill. No, our whole family got complete physicals a few months ago when Michael's office got a new health-care provider. We are both in perfect health. I guess he's just lost interest in me. You know, that's why I started to teach aerobics last year. I thought that maybe he was bored with a wife who stayed home and kept the kids and the house in order. It hasn't helped anything."

"Are you nuts? Of course it's helped. You're the most gorgeous, physically fit woman I know."

"You're sweet. Thanks, Sally."

"I have to tell you, though, it upsets me to think that you'd go back to work to try to interest Michael. What about you, Juliet? Forget about trying to please Michael. What makes you happy that has nothing to do with being a wife or even a mother?"

"I guess I've been so obsessed with trying to win Michael back these past few years, I've forgotten about everything else."

"Well, I'm no psychologist, but everything I've heard and read over the years seems to indicate that one of the biggest problems that can happen to a homemaker is to lose her sense of herself. To forget the person she was before she had a husband or family. If a woman does that, then they say she goes through a real depression when her kids grow up and leave home."

"My girls are way too young to leave home, but I've been semi-depressed for years."

"I'm so sorry, Juliet. I wish you had felt comfortable sharing this with me before now. I couldn't have changed anything, but sometimes just talking about your discouragement can help."

"Actually, I think teaching the Dancercise classes helps me not feel so depressed. It just hasn't made Michael more attracted to me."

"But I think he is attracted to you. It's obvious to me that he really loves you."

"I think he loves me. I just don't know what's wrong . . . or how to reach him. Sometimes days will go by and I'll realize that we haven't even kissed each other good night. I'll tell him that we haven't hugged or kissed for a long time, and he'll give me a nice little brotherly peck on the cheek. I've just about given up. It's embarrassing to have to tell your husband that he hasn't kissed you in over a week."

"Do you think he's depressed about anything?"

"He had a hard time dealing with his dad's death, and I think he's wondering if he really wants to be in real estate for the rest of his life. But what can I do about that?"

"Pray."

"You're right. This is definitely more than I can handle. God needs to show me what to do. What about you and John? Have you ever gone through dry spells in your marriage?"

"John and I have had our share of problems with money and in-laws and stuff, but thankfully sex has never been a problem."

"Now I'm even more depressed. I wonder if I'm the only woman in the whole world whose husband thinks that making love with her is an imposition."

"Now don't go feeling sorry for yourself. That's not going to help anything. You know, Juliet, the older I get, the more I realize that every single person has some issue that dogs them. Life is never perfect. There have been times in our marriage when I would have been thankful if our only problem had been a lack of sex drive. Like the time right after Katie was born and John was out of work for a year."

"Oh, Sally, I know. I must sound like an ungrateful brat. We've never had any really scary problems like no money or bad health. The thing that makes this so hard for me, I think, is that Michael was so attentive and romantic in the early years of our marriage. He hopelessly spoiled me by being such an incredible lover. And then one day, it was all gone."

"Juliet, I don't know how to help you, but I will warn you that I think it's a trap to waste your time living in the past. So your past with Michael was more romantic and fulfilling than your present. The past is over. Be thankful that you had a happy start to your marriage, but don't get stuck there."

As the waitress stopped at their table to refill their coffee cups, Sally looked over at Juliet and shook her head with an amazed expression on her face. She waited for the waitress to move on to another table, then said, "This is so obvious, I can't believe I haven't thought of it before."

"What? What's obvious?" Juliet asked hopefully.

"Have you ever just asked Michael why he doesn't want to make love? Have you asked him if he thinks he's impotent? Because I've seen on the news that they have medicine now that can fix that problem."

Juliet was horrified. "Are you serious? I'd never ask him anything like that! It's far too personal."

"Juliet, we're talking about your husband, not a checkout clerk at the grocery store. I think it's completely appropriate for you to talk to him about his sexuality. He's your lover."

"Well, he used to be. But Sally, I think that would only do more harm than good. I mean, if he is impotent, I'd just make him feel miserable by bringing up the subject. And if he isn't, I'd be insulting him by suggesting it. Maybe an insult like that could make him become impotent, if he isn't already."

"Now there's where I think you've got it all wrong. You

seem to think it's insulting to wonder if a man is impotent. Do you think it's insulting to ask a friend if she's gone through menopause yet? To me, these are just the realities of our human condition."

"I'd never ask a girlfriend if she was going through menopause. Maybe I'm just more puritanical than the average person, but I think both those topics are far too personal."

"Maybe . . . but not for a wife to ask her husband. Look at it this way, Juliet. You are painfully aware of this issue in your marriage. No doubt Michael is equally aware of the problem. Why not just clear the air by talking with him about it?"

"Because even the thought of talking about it terrifies me. I just sense that, with Michael, this topic is taboo. You mentioned that time in your marriage when John was out of work for a year. Did you ever talk to him about being unemployed during that scary time?"

"Of course. That was practically all we talked about for most of that year. 'When do you think you'll have a job again?' and 'How are we going to make it financially?'"

"But didn't that just make John feel more discouraged?"

"I don't think so. I think he was relieved to be able to talk to me about the stress and the fear he was feeling. Juliet, I think husbands and wives should be able to talk freely about anything that affects their lives, don't you?"

"I guess I've never had that kind of openness with Michael. Not as completely as you're describing it. Maybe it's my fault because I do sense that I'm kind of a prude, but especially when it comes to private topics like sex, I've always been very shy."

"I just think it seems like the obvious thing to do, to ask Michael why he can't or won't make love to you, but you know him much better than I ever will."

"Sally, I'll think about what you've said, but right now I'm just tired of the whole subject." She sighed and shook her head. "Thank you for skipping the meeting and for letting me dump all this depressing stuff on you."

"Juliet, you're like a sister to me. I'm always happy to talk to you about anything. You know that."

When they met back at their room later that afternoon, Michael didn't say anything about the men's meeting. Juliet was dying to know what they had talked about and was hoping Michael would want to order room service for dinner, like Sally and John were planning to do, but Michael had other plans.

"I noticed when we were driving to the hotel last night that the new *Star Trek* movie is showing right down the street from here. Why don't we grab a burger or something and see it?"

"Really? That's what you want to do?"

"Well, yeah. If we wait to see it when we get back home, we'll just have to hire a sitter. I think we should see it tonight."

Juliet's emotions were so numb and she felt so drained

from crying and talking to Sally that she figured it probably was a good idea. They could sit together in the dark and wouldn't have to go through the effort of trying to think of something to say to each other.

The next day, as they drove back to Jessica's house to get their girls, Michael asked Juliet if she had enjoyed the conference.

"You were right, Michael. It was a waste of time. They just told us things I've heard or read about before. I'm sorry that I dragged you away from your appointments this weekend."

"I'm sorry you were disappointed with the seminar. I liked going to the movie last night."

And that's the way they left it. Sally had made an impression on Juliet when she told her that every person and every marriage has some sort of problem they just have to live with. Sally was right; it was dangerous to live in the past and to feel sorry for herself. Juliet was tired of acting like a whiny, self-pitying baby. She decided it was time to grow up and get on with things.

Late that night, after she had unpacked their suitcases and the girls and Michael were long asleep, Juliet decided to make her decision to let go of this problem official. She took Heathcliff out on the deck behind the living room and sat on the porch swing with an afghan wrapped around her shoulders. The loyal dog curled up at her feet and fell asleep. She looked up into the clear, dark sky, bursting with stars, and talked to God.

"Oh, Father, will you please forgive me for focusing so

much on what's wrong in my marriage and forgetting to thank you for all the ways you've blessed me? When I think of how much I have and how unthankful I've been, I am so ashamed. How could I have taken everything for granted? You've blessed me again and again, and all I've done lately is complain. Please forgive me.

"Lord, I'm turning this problem with Michael over to you. I'm tired of trying to fix something that I can't even understand, and I'm tired of being miserable. I was happy for twenty-one years without a sex life, and I can be happy again if I have to live without it. From now on, I'm leaving this whole mess in your hands. Thank you for taking care of it for me."

A feeling that she hadn't felt for longer than she could remember filled Juliet's heart. It was peace. She didn't know how everything was going to turn out, and she didn't have to know anymore. Her life and her marriage were in God's hands. She smiled to herself and marveled at how such a simple thing as a prayer could make such a difference.

A gentle paw rested on her foot, and she looked down into the sincere brown eyes of her most devoted friend. "Heathcliff, do you have any idea how precious you are to me? Where would I be without your love?" She knelt down on the deck next to her dog and hugged him as he thumped his tail and licked her on the cheek. Then they went back into the dark house together and raced one another up the stairs to Juliet and Michael's bedroom.

Careful not to wake her sleeping husband, Juliet crawled

under the comforter and patted the empty space next to her on the outside edge of the king-sized bed. Heathcliff jumped up on the bed, plastered himself against her legs, and settled down to sleep. With a deep sigh, Juliet let the frustrations and disappointments of the past two days go. God was taking care of it.

Chapter Seven

Michael reluctantly agreed to spend that Thanksgiving at the Parkers' cabin near Lake Tahoe with Jessica and Dan's family, but he insisted on going in separate cars. Juliet wanted to leave on Wednesday afternoon, right after the girls got out of school, and stay at Lake Tahoe until Sunday night. Michael said he had to work on Wednesday. He planned to leave at dawn on Thanksgiving morning so that he'd be at the cabin by the early afternoon. Then he would have to leave on Friday afternoon so he could work all day Saturday. The only thing that appealed to Juliet about his plan was that she wouldn't have to find anyone to take care of Sheba since the cat would be alone for less than two days. Heathcliff was going with them.

Daisy and Heather were eager to go when their mom came to pick them up at school on Wednesday afternoon.

Juliet wanted to get on the road as soon as possible, so she had packed the trunk of her Cadillac the night before. She thought it was a shame that they weren't traveling as a family. It not only would have been nice to share the driving but also she would have enjoyed being able to visit with Michael without the distractions of the TV and telephone.

It bothered her that Daisy and Heather spent so little time really talking with their dad. He worked late many evenings, and often he would call and tell her not to hold dinner for him. She would save something for him to reheat in the microwave when he got home, but it didn't seem right that they didn't spend more time together as a family. When he did come home earlier in the evening, usually most of his time was spent on the phone. By the time he was done calling people, it was the children's bedtime, and he would plop down on his recliner to watch *Star Trek* reruns.

Juliet didn't need anyone to tell her that this was a setup for a dysfunctional family. As a little girl growing up, she had always enjoyed dinnertime in her home. Some of her sweetest childhood memories involved happy times around the dining-room table with her parents and her sister. But she was determined not to nag at Michael or to make him feel guilty for not giving his family a higher priority. Juliet hoped that if she was the best, most devoted mom she could possibly be that somehow this would make up for the gaps left by Michael's neglectful parenting. And since her talk with Sally during the marriage enrichment weekend, she was making a real effort not to complain when life wasn't going exactly the way she wanted it to.

Juliet stopped by her sister's house first, so that Jessica's daughter, Rachel, could ride with her cousins. Juliet would follow Dan on the drive to Tahoe, and they'd stop together for dinner in Sacramento. Bumper-to-bumper traffic jammed the highways leaving San Jose. As Juliet inched along in her car, trying not to lose sight of Dan's red Toyota station wagon, she promised herself that she would do everything in her power to make the little time she was going to have with Michael enjoyable.

Heathcliff was sleeping next to her on the white leather bench seat, his head resting on her lap. The three little girls in the back seat, who had been having a sing-along all the way from Scott's Valley to San Jose, were getting restless as the traffic slowed down. They wanted to know when they would be stopping to eat and how much longer it would take to get to the mountains. Juliet put Vivaldi's *Four Seasons* in the CD player and tried to tune out the irritations from the back seat as she settled in for the long drive to Tahoe.

It was very late when she parked her Cadillac next to Dan's car in the dirt lot in front of the dark cabin. The three little girls were asleep in the back of Juliet's car, as were the Parkers' two boys in the back of their car. The parents decided to let the kids stay in the cars while they unloaded everything and Dan got a fire going in the wood-burning stove.

Juliet stepped out of her car and quickly reached back

in to pull out her down jacket. No snow covered the ground yet, but the children were hoping to have a chance for sledding before the weekend was over. Heathcliff jumped out of the car, happy to be free to run, and Juliet walked around the yard with him for a few minutes. It felt so good to stretch her legs and to breathe the fresh, cold, pine air.

Jessica offered to let Juliet and Michael have the big master bedroom and connecting bath on the first floor of the house, but Juliet wouldn't hear of it. Michael was only going to be there for one night, and she wanted Dan and her sister to have more privacy. She took the smaller bedroom upstairs, with a double bed. Next to it was a large, dormer-type bedroom with three sets of bunk beds for the children. Jessica and Juliet had helped all the kids change into warm sweat suits when they had stopped for dinner in Sacramento. Now they simply led the half-asleep children up the stairs and tucked them into their beds.

Dan was exhausted and planned to be the first one up the next morning to start the wood-burning stove so he went to bed right after the kids. Juliet and Jessica sat in the living room next to the cozy stove and drank hot apple cider while they planned how they'd get their Thanksgiving cooking underway the next morning. The two sisters hadn't had any private moments since the marriage enrichment conference the month before, so Jessica asked how it had gone. When Juliet shrugged indifferently, Jessica asked, "So you don't think it was worth the time and the money?"

"You and Dan might enjoy going to a conference like

that some day; Sally and John had a wonderful weekend, and that was their third one. It just wasn't a good fit for Michael and me. I wouldn't want to go to another one."

"Do you think it helped your marriage? I've been worried about you and Michael since we talked that day."

"Don't worry about us. You were probably right when you said a couple couldn't expect to be on their honeymoon for the rest of their lives. I guess it's just time for me to grow up."

Juliet felt freezing cold, even with flannel sheets on the bed, when she finally crawled under the covers and tried to fall asleep. Heathcliff was right next to her legs, and the two tossed and turned until Juliet was finally able to warm up under all the blankets and get comfortable in the strange bed. She lay in the darkness, listening to an owl hooting outside the window and remembering the times she and Michael had shared this room in the past. They had made many trips to the cabin over the years, both before and after the girls had been born. It had always been a refreshing break for them. She was hoping that it would be that way again.

The next morning Juliet woke up and saw on her travel alarm that it was already nine o'clock. She could smell the wonderful fragrance of burning pine logs in the wood stove combined with the scent of cinnamon rolls and coffee in the kitchen. She figured that Jessica must be up if the rolls were in the oven. Feeling guilty for sleeping so late, Juliet quickly dressed in her jeans and a sapphire blue turtleneck and hurried downstairs to help.

When she walked into the kitchen, she was surprised that her sister wasn't anywhere in sight. Dan had gathered the five children at the big kitchen table and was helping them put butter on their cinnamon rolls and pour glasses of orange juice.

"Dan, how sweet of you! Thank you for getting breakfast for the kids. Is Jessie still asleep?"

"Yes. I know you girls have a big day of cooking ahead, and I thought you'd enjoy the extra sleep. I made a fresh pot of coffee. Why don't you grab a cup and have a cinnamon roll while they're still hot?"

"That sounds great. I'll just take Heathcliff outside and be right back for some."

"Don't worry about Heathcliff. Danny was the first one up this morning, and he and I took Heathcliff for a walk about an hour ago. After breakfast, I've promised to take all the kids on a real hike, and we'd like Heathcliff to come with us, if that's okay with you."

"I'm sure he'd enjoy that much more than watching me cook. Thank you, Dan. It isn't often that I wake up and find my kids already fed and my dog already walked. You're an angel!"

After the children finished eating and Dan had left with them for their hike, Juliet poured herself a second mug of coffee and sat back down at the table, lost in thought. Jessica came out of her bedroom a few minutes later, poured her own coffee, and joined her sister.

"Hi, Jessie. Did you know that your husband built the fire this morning, made the breakfast, walked my dog, and now he has all the kids and Heathcliff out for a hike? Has he always been this helpful?"

"Isn't he great? He's a wonderful father and a pretty devoted husband, too."

"But has he always been like that?"

"Yeah, I think so. I don't ever remember asking him to help me with the kids or the house. He just sees what needs to be done and pitches in."

"That must be wonderful."

The sisters didn't have much time to sit at the table with their coffee. A lot of cooking awaited them. They had brought all the things they'd need to make the Thanksgiving meal with them so that they wouldn't have to grocery shop as well.

The roasting turkey had begun to fill the cabin with a delicious aroma when Juliet heard Michael's car pull up to the front of the house. She put down the mixing bowl she was washing and rushed to the front door to greet him. Daisy and Heather had been playing cards with their uncle Dan and their cousins on the living-room floor, but the two girls jumped up when they heard their daddy come in. "Daddy, Daddy!" They rushed over to him, and he lifted them up, one at a time, for a hug and a kiss.

"How was the drive up?" Juliet asked as she walked over and kissed Michael on the cheek.

"It was fine. I'm tired, though. I was up at five this morning. Do you think I have time for a nap before we eat dinner?"

Juliet stopped herself before she could complain about

him walking in the door and going straight to bed. It was true that the drive up was exhausting. She had wanted to go right to sleep when they had arrived the night before. She ignored the fact that she wished he would stay up and visit with all of them. Instead, she smiled at him as he went upstairs to their bedroom.

The sun had already set when the Parkers and the Nelsons gathered around the big kitchen table for their abundant Thanksgiving feast. Dan led them in a prayer of thanks before they sat down at the table to eat. Juliet and Jessica hadn't skipped any of the traditional side dishes. They had roast turkey with giblet gravy, mashed potatoes, cornbread stuffing, candied sweet potatoes, green bean casserole, cranberry sauce, deviled eggs, stuffed celery, black olives, and hot rolls and butter. For dessert they made cherry and pumpkin and chocolate cream pies. Tears filled Juliet's eyes as she looked around the table and counted her blessings.

After the meal, the kids went to the living room to watch *The Wizard of Oz* on TV while the adults lingered around the table with their cups of coffee. Dan and Michael were talking about which football teams they thought would make it to the Super Bowl that year, and Jessica turned to Juliet, who was dishing out another slice of chocolate pie for herself. "It's not fair that you can eat that much and keep that figure of yours."

"I think I've inherited Dad's fast metabolism. He's always eaten anything he wants and has never been overweight."

"I've been thinking about this for a long time, Julie, ever since I had Danny and gained ten pounds that have refused to come off. I've inherited Mom's weight struggles and Dad's coloring, and you've inherited Mom's dark Italian looks and Dad's metabolism. Want to trade?"

"Don't be silly. You're beautiful, Jessie. So what if you've added a pound or two? You've had three kids in ten years."

"You've had two kids in eight years and have never changed your size since high school. I miss being able to eat what I want."

"I'm sure I take it for granted, Jessie. I can't imagine having to be on a diet. I don't think I have enough self-discipline."

After Juliet and Jessica had cleaned up the kitchen and put the kids to bed, Dan suggested that they soak in the hot tub out on the enclosed deck. A few Christmases before, Dan and his siblings all had chipped in to surprise their parents with the luxury. It was a sensual indulgence to soak in the steamy tub after a long hike or a day on the ski slopes. Dan had been preparing the tub since early that morning so that it would be hot and ready to use after the Thanksgiving dinner.

Juliet thought it was a heavenly idea; her legs and back were stiff from standing at the kitchen counter most of the day. She was surprised and disappointed to hear Michael declining. He hadn't brought a swimsuit, and he wanted to go to bed early. The long drive up had worn him out, and he still had a big weekend ahead of him. Juliet decided to bow out, too. If Michael didn't want to soak, she wanted to give her sister and brother-in-law some time alone.

A little later, Juliet sat propped up in bed, reading next to Michael, who was already sound asleep. She had intentionally saved the latest murder mystery by her favorite author for this holiday. She knew there was a good possibility that Dan and her sister would want to be by themselves after the kids were in bed at night, and she wanted to have a great, distracting book to keep her company.

Years before, her favorite books had been romance novels, but in recent years she had switched to mysteries. Reading a romance novel these days was like rubbing salt into a wound. Now, as she tried to concentrate on the mystery, she found that her mind constantly wandered.

Jessica and Dan were soaking in the hot tub on the deck below Michael and Juliet's bedroom window. Juliet could hear them talking softly and laughing, and she remembered a time long ago when she and Michael had enjoyed each other's company. She looked at her sleeping husband, snoring softly. It took every ounce of willpower she had to kill the self-pity that was welling up inside her.

Chapter Eight

Michael was the first one up the next morning, and he started a fire in the wood stove and put on a pot of coffee. When the coffee had brewed, he poured himself some and went outside to sit on a bench in front of the cabin while Heathcliff wandered around the yard, sniffing every tree and patch of weeds.

Michael could sense Juliet's disappointment, in fact he knew she had been unhappy for years, but he didn't know what to do about it. She seemed to have a great need to share every thought and feeling, and her romantic expectations had been a burden to him for a long time. She acted as if love and romance were the only important things in life. He wished life could be that easy.

Michael felt as if he were being swallowed alive by the pressure to keep his family intact financially. For years now, the real estate market had been depressed, and it had taken every ounce of his ingenuity to keep his family from losing their house and every other comfortable convenience they had come to enjoy. He never shared any of the stress he was under with Juliet. He believed it was a man's job to provide for his family. A real man didn't go running and whining to his wife about every little pressure he faced at work.

When Juliet and Michael were first married and the real estate market seemed to be going nowhere but up, they had gotten into a habit of casually spending lots of money for luxuries, such as new cars every other year and new wardrobes every season. He didn't want to change any of their spending habits and alert his wife to the financial mess they were in, so their debts continued to grow. Now when he looked at their bills, he didn't know how they would ever dig out of the hole they were in. All he could do was work like a fiend and pray that someday they would be in the black again.

He knew that Juliet was disappointed in their nonexistent love life. His lack of sex drive surprised and disturbed him, too. From the first day he'd met Juliet, she was all he ever wanted. In the early years of their marriage, they had enjoyed a completely fulfilling and passionate physical closeness. She was perfect for him in every way, yet now he never felt the desire to make love with her. She still appealed to him physically, but he had simply lost all interest in sex somewhere during the past few years of financial torment. All he could think about anymore was how he and his family were going to survive the financial mess they were in. How could he explain to his wife that his only real passion these days was for making money? He brought Heathcliff back inside and found Juliet in the kitchen, beating eggs in a bowl for French toast.

"Hi! You're up early," Juliet said with a smile. "Thanks for walking Heathcliff for me."

"It's beautiful up here, isn't it?" His wife was beautiful too, Michael thought, as he watched her fixing the French toast. She had a fresh, natural beauty. Even dressed in an old sweat suit, with no makeup, and with her hair pulled back in a simple ponytail, she was the prettiest girl in the world to him. How he'd love to tell her that and to assure her that he still loved her. It concerned him sometimes to think how frustrated she must be by his neglect of her physical desires. But it was worse to be affectionate toward her. If he did that, she'd want to make love, and he knew he'd only let her down.

She looked over at Michael with an appeal in her amazing blue eyes. "Are you sure you have to leave today? It seems like you just got here."

"I know. I did just get here. But a couple from Virginia is being transferred to Santa Cruz in January, and they'll be in town this weekend to house hunt with me."

"I hope you earn a big fat commission to make up for our missing you."

"So do I, Juliet. So do I . . ."

Michael had a nice breakfast with everyone and walked down to the lake with the kids before he got into his BMW and headed back to Mount Hermon and his private hell.

The children got their wish on Saturday morning when they woke up to two feet of new snow. They could hardly wait to eat breakfast and take their sleds out to the hill behind the cabin. All day, they trooped in and out the front door. First they would warm up next to the wood stove with cups of hot chocolate and dry off a little, then they would dress up again in all their snow gear and trudge back up the hill with their sleds.

That night, after everyone soaked in the hot tub, Dan offered to read to the kids and tuck them all into bed. Jessica said good night and exchanged a secret smile with Dan as he walked up the stairs behind the kids. Juliet looked at her sister suspiciously and said, "Okay, Jessie. I know that look of yours. What's up?"

"You caught me. I do have something planned. Do you remember awhile ago when we were reminiscing about our growing up years? You said some of your favorite memories were of the Saturday nights when we would watch old movies on TV after Mom and Dad had gone to bed."

Juliet smiled as she thought of those happy times. "That was the best, wasn't it? Those nights always made me happy to have you for my sister."

As she walked to her bedroom, Jessica called over her shoulder, "Well, just wait a minute. I have something special for you." She came back out with a wrapped present in her hand and gave it to Juliet.

"What's this? What's the occasion?"

"This is an early Christmas gift. Open it."

Juliet gasped as she ripped off the shiny gold bow and wrapping paper to reveal a copy of the classic movie *Wuthering Heights.* "Oh, Jessie! What a thoughtful surprise."

"Did I remember right? Is it still your favorite?"

"I've never loved any movie more than *Wuthering Heights.* I even named my dog Heathcliff." Hearing his name, the exhausted Border collie, who had chased the children up and down the snowy hill all day, came over and plopped down at Juliet's feet. "I haven't seen this movie since before I married Michael."

"Do you want to get some coffee and pie and watch it with me?" Jessica asked, heading toward the kitchen.

"Are you kidding? Of course I do!" Just as they had done years ago, the two sisters got their bed pillows and blankets and snacks and settled on the floor in front of the TV together to watch the tragic love story.

Juliet was openly crying when the final credits rolled. Jessica handed her another tissue and took one for herself. "Julie, this was supposed to cheer you up. Maybe I should have bought *Bringing Up Baby* instead."

"Oh no, Jessie. I still love *Wuthering Heights;* it's a beautiful story. And I am cheered to think you'd go to all this trouble to surprise me." She blew her nose and shook her head. "That speech that Heathcliff said at Cathy's deathbed just destroyed me. 'I cannot live without my life. I cannot die without my soul.' Can you imagine having someone love you like that?"

"Julie! Thank God neither of us has a love like that. They both died tragic deaths, and I don't think they were ever really happy."

"But Heathcliff remained passionately in love with Cathy, even after her death. He never grew tired of her or took her for granted."

"Oh, I see. You're thinking of Michael. Julie, if you're so unhappy with the way things are in your marriage that you're starting to envy people on their deathbeds, this should be a sign to you that you need some help."

"Jessie, I know that Hollywood glamorizes love and doesn't show life or love very realistically. I don't think it's unrealistic, though, to want my husband to still be interested in me. You and Dan have been married longer than Michael and me, and Dan is still thoughtful and considerate. It was so sweet of him to set up the hot tub the other day so that you could soak after a long day of cooking."

"Don't get trapped into comparing what you have with what somebody else has. I probably do take Dan and his loving ways for granted; he's a darling man. But I could compare myself to you and feel envious. I'd love to trade my extra pounds for your perfect body, or trade my normal house for your near mansion."

"It's just that love has always been the most important thing in the world to me. When I met Michael, I believed he was my own Heathcliff. Remember how amazing he was when I was engaged to him and when we were first married?"

"Well, I'm sure that even a successful real estate agent like Michael doesn't have enough money to continue to spoil you lavishly for the rest of your life."

"No, Jessie. I'm not talking about spoiling me with things that cost money. I'm talking about the way he used to lavish me with his love, with himself."

"Look, will you do me a favor and at least think about getting some counseling with Michael? Maybe you could sort your problems out if you would talk with your pastor."

"Maybe. At the moment though, I think I need to give Michael a break. Last month I dragged him to the marriage conference, and this month I made him come here for Thanksgiving, and he didn't seem to enjoy either one. I think I need to leave him alone for a while."

After everyone had gone to bed Saturday night, another foot of snow fell. When they woke up Sunday morning, the adults voted unanimously to leave right after breakfast so they could drive home during daylight hours. But it was time-consuming to pack everything, shovel out the snow behind and on top of their cars, and close up the cabin. The water to the house had to be shut off so the pipes wouldn't freeze, and they wanted to leave the cabin neat and clean.

Even with everyone pitching in, it took hours to finish all the chores that needed to be done. On the refrigerator door, Dan's parents had posted a checklist of things to do before a family left after a vacation. It was understood that anyone who borrowed the cabin would wash and change the sheets on the beds, vacuum or wash the floors, wash all the dishes and put them away, empty the refrigerator and the trash cans, and clean the bathrooms. By the time the last item was checked off the list, the kids were hungry again. Jessica and Juliet quickly fixed peanut butter and jelly sandwiches for everyone, and finally they were on the road.

Juliet desperately wished that she and Michael had come to Lake Tahoe in the same car. The snow that had seemed so pretty and entertaining while the kids were sledding down the hill the day before was terrifying as Juliet tried to drive in it. She had been to Lake Tahoe in the past when it was snowy, but Michael had always done the driving. Now she suddenly had to come to grips with the knowledge that she had absolutely no experience driving on icy roads.

It seemed to take forever just to get through the little Tahoma subdivision and onto the main road that circled Lake Tahoe. As her car skidded along the deserted neighborhood streets, Juliet told herself that as soon as she got to the main road, the driving would get easier. But a minute on the main road convinced a dismayed Juliet that it was just as impossible as the streets in the subdivision. As far as she could tell, the snowplows hadn't cleared the roads once since the storm began. She was terrified to feel her car slipping and sliding.

Juliet's hands started to tingle, and she realized that she

was gripping the steering wheel so tightly, her hands had gotten numb. Her Cadillac had good, all-weather tires, but they didn't seem to be helping her in these conditions. She yelled out in terror a few times when she tried to stop the car and it fishtailed. Dan was driving ahead of her in his little Toyota Tercel, but it had four-wheel drive, and he seemed to be doing fine.

Finally, he pulled off the road into a mini-market parking lot and asked Juliet if she was doing okay. She was so terrified, she was almost in tears. Dan suggested that they put chains on her tires until they got to a section of the highway with clearer pavement.

As Juliet watched her brother-in-law kneeling in the freezing snow and putting the chains on her tires, she felt a sudden flash of anger at Michael. Why wasn't her own husband here to help her? Would the world have ended if he had missed another day or two of work? He was so focused on making money that he was abandoning his family when they really needed him. She understood how it must feel to be a single parent. But that thought only made her more angry. She wasn't a single parent. Her husband was just never there for her anymore.

The drive from Tahoma to Colfax took more than four hours. Juliet couldn't drive any faster than twenty-five miles an hour with the chains on, and at times, she had to completely stop because of all the cars scattered across the road from accidents. It took almost two hours to cross the Donner Summit because so many cars had spun out on Highway 80. Juliet was relieved to finally reach Colfax, where she was able to pull over again and have Dan take the chains off her tires. She was very quiet during the rest of the long drive to Mount Hermon. Rachel, Daisy, and Heather fell asleep after they stopped for an early dinner in Sacramento.

As Juliet searched her heart in the silence of the car, she knew that she needed to make an attitude adjustment before she got back home. The anger she held toward Michael was irrational. She reasoned with herself that no one knew when they made their Thanksgiving plans that Juliet was going to have to drive alone on slippery, snowy roads. Snow hadn't even been predicted before they left Mount Hermon on Wednesday. She knew that Michael would have wanted to help her if he could have. In fact, if he hadn't been so conscientious about maintaining her car, she wouldn't have had chains in the trunk.

She reminded herself again that she needed to grow up and stop complaining when things went wrong. How many families would love to take their children to a beautiful cabin at Lake Tahoe for the weekend? She had been privileged to enjoy the holiday with her darling children and her sister's family. And what a blessing it was to have a sister like Jessica, who was a loving friend as well as a devoted sister. When she finally returned to Mount Hermon and Michael, she was almost able to be civil.

Chapter Nine

Suddenly Christmas was upon them. Juliet was looking forward to a visit from her mother-in-law. Leah planned to fly out from New York on December 20 and stay until the New Year. Juliet would be hosting the Christmas Day dinner at her house, but her father wouldn't be joining them. He had taken a year's sabbatical from teaching and had gone to Stratford-upon-Avon. He was overjoyed to be staying in the town where Shakespeare was born and would be doing some extensive studying at the Shakespeare Centre.

Usually the Nelsons eagerly anticipated the Christmas season. On the first Saturday in December, they would go high into the Santa Cruz Mountains and cut down their Christmas tree. Then they would decorate both the tree and the house with the beautiful, sentimental ornaments that Juliet had been collecting since she was a little girl. Most years, Michael would be the first one to jump out of bed, put on a pot of coffee, and get the girls up and going for their Christmas tree expedition. This year, he didn't seem to have it in him to even try to be enthusiastic about their yearly outing. He wasn't grouchy—just preoccupied and somewhat disinterested in the whole process. Even the girls seemed to notice his unusual response to something he had always enjoyed.

"Daddy, you seem sad. Aren't you glad we're getting a tree?" Daisy asked him as they drove toward Highway 17.

"Sure I am, Daisy. Do you think you'll be strong enough to saw our tree down this year all by yourself?"

Heather, never willing to be outdone by her big sister, piped in, "I bet I'm strong enough, Daddy."

"Well, you can both try. Your dad's getting too old to cut down Christmas trees."

That comment got Juliet thinking as they traveled along the familiar hairpin turns leading to the tree farm. Michael was going to be forty-three in February. She'd often heard people talking about men and their midlife crises, and now she wondered if Michael's age could have any bearing on his weariness for life. Then she reminded herself that Michael's problems, whatever they were, belonged to him and to God. It was no longer her business to fuss and fret and analyze every comment the poor man made. She had been feeling better since she had prayed that night after the marriage enrichment weekend, and she didn't want to go back to her neurotic obsessions. It was time to think about something else.

"Hey, girls, what kind of tree do we want to get this year?" Juliet asked as they arrived at the tree farm.

"I want the kind with the blue needles," Daisy said with conviction.

"I want a great big one that will touch the top of the ceiling," added Heather.

After trekking through the trees and much debating and negotiating, they all agreed on a seven-foot blue spruce that nearly touched the ceiling in front of the French doors in their living room. Michael helped Juliet anchor the tree in the metal stand and then hurried off to meet someone who wanted to see a house. The girls helped their mom trim the tree with tiny white lights, red velvet bows, and the delightful assortment of ornaments.

When Michael returned for dinner that evening, his daughters met him at the garage door. They insisted that he cover his eyes as they led him into the living room, lit only by the lights from the tree. He congratulated them on their lovely decorating job, and they went into the kitchen to eat some of Juliet's homemade chicken potpie.

In keeping with Sally's advice to start doing things again that she used to enjoy and let God take care of Michael, the next week Juliet decided to take the girls with her to San Francisco for a weekend of shopping. She and Michael had gone there for Christmas shopping a couple times before the girls had been born, and it had never failed to put her in the spirit of the holiday.

As she expected, Michael didn't want to take a weekend off from work. Also, Juliet felt that she had learned an important lesson after the fiasco of talking him into spending a little time with them during Thanksgiving. If

Michael didn't want to go somewhere with them as a family, they'd probably have more fun leaving him at home.

Daisy and Heather, on the other hand, were delighted with the idea of sleeping at a hotel, riding the cable cars, and visiting Santa Claus. She and the girls packed up the car on Friday afternoon, two weeks before Christmas, and stopped by Michael's office with last-minute instructions about Heathcliff.

"Michael, will you please be sure to stay in the yard with Heathcliff when you let him out to go to the bathroom? He's really become attached to me, and I'm worried that he might get nervous because I'm gone and come looking for me."

"Juliet, he's going to be fine. You've watched *Homeward Bound* too many times. Just go and have fun."

"I've already given both of the pets their dinners. And I've put the phone number for the Holiday Inn on the refrigerator in case there's a problem." She always hated to leave her dog behind. Michael was right. She probably shouldn't have watched *Homeward Bound* so often over the years. The movie about the cat and two dogs finding their misplaced owners was one of her favorites, even though it always made her cry and definitely fed her obsession about their pets.

"Will you just go and have a good time? Everything's going to be fine." Michael's voice sounded slightly exasperated. She knew that sometimes her preoccupation with the pets got on his nerves. Juliet had brought Heathcliff home as a puppy three years earlier and had been off the deep end about him ever since. He was the first dog either of them had adopted. As far as Michael was concerned, dogs were too much trouble, even though he admitted that Heathcliff was a very intelligent, loyal animal. Sheba was a better fit for him. She was cute when he wanted to pet her, and self-sufficient when he was too busy to bother. The phone at Michael's desk rang, and he waved Juliet and the girls off with a distracted smile as he talked to the client on the other end of the line.

As Juliet and the girls drove north on Highway 1 toward San Francisco, she was glad she had decided to go. The radio station played Christmas carols, and the three of them sang along as the sun set over the Pacific Ocean. The traffic became bumper-to-bumper when they took the off-ramp from the freeway into the city, and Juliet was very tense as she tried to find her way to Union Square. She was so relieved to finally locate the hotel's parking garage and leave her car behind for the weekend.

When they drove past Union Square, Daisy immediately noticed the ice-skating rink and began to plead with her mom. She was still pestering her about it when they took their bags up to the room. "Mom, Heather and I have only roller-skated. We've never ice-skated yet. We have to try it."

"Well, sweetheart, I'd like to try ice-skating too, but can we do that on Sunday morning instead of tonight? I think we wouldn't be so cold that way. Also, I am really hungry. I was busy getting us all packed this afternoon, and I skipped lunch."

"Why can't we skate tomorrow morning?"

"Remember, girls, the main reason we came here was to get our Christmas shopping done. We can skate on Sunday right before we leave for home. That way, if it makes me really sore, I won't have a whole day of shopping ahead of me."

They went downstairs for a quick dinner of soup and sandwiches in the hotel's café, and then they ventured out to examine all the elaborately decorated and animated Christmas window displays in the stores around Union Square. The next morning, they were up early to ride a cable car down to Pier 39. They found a very realistic stuffed mouse for Sheba at Kitty City, and the girls picked out some special keepsake ornaments for themselves at Santa's Workshop. Juliet wanted them to start their own ornament collections, just as she had when she was their age. After that, she was ready to take a break so she let the girls ride on the carousel while she sat and watched from a bench.

Later, while they were eating clam chowder and sourdough French bread at a café on Pier 39 and watching the sea lions, Daisy surprised Juliet with a question. "Mommy, why doesn't Daddy like to be with us anymore?"

"Why do you think that, Daisy?" Juliet tried to keep her voice casual, but she was disturbed to think her daughter felt Michael's neglect.

"He didn't come with us this weekend, and he didn't have fun last Saturday when we got our tree."

"Honey, he always has to work on the weekends, and he

really doesn't like to shop as much as we do. I think we tire him out when we make him Christmas shop with us."

"Yeah. I remember last year when we made him go Christmas shopping with us. He spent most of the time drinking coffee at Burger King."

Juliet smiled at the memory her daughter evoked. "Maybe one of the nicest gifts we can give Daddy this year is to not make him shop too much."

"I like shopping. Mommy, are we going to see Santa Claus now?" Heather had been very patient all morning, but now lunch was over, and she had been put off long enough.

"Yes, darling. It's time to get back on the cable car so we can go to Macy's and find Santa."

As Juliet drove back home Sunday afternoon, she realized that she still had many more Christmas gifts to buy, but she was so glad they had gone for their special girls' weekend. Daisy and Heather would have some happy memories of their time with her, and Juliet had a whole list of gift ideas for the girls after seeing what they had liked at the many stores they had visited.

She wondered if the old saying, Absence makes the heart grow fonder, was true after all. Juliet had thought of Michael so often during the past two days, especially at dinner the night before. She and the girls had gone to Chinatown late on Saturday afternoon to get freshwater pearl necklaces for Jessica and her mother-in-law. After poking through some interesting little gift shops and finding two perfect necklaces, they went to a Chinese restaurant that Juliet and Michael had loved years before. The food was wonderful, but the sweet memories of her husband and the fun they had together were even better.

So much of what she had done with the girls that weekend was a retracing of the past. At times her heart was almost overflowing with loving remembrances of the wonderful man she had married. As she drove through Santa Cruz, she decided that she would make a new commitment to love Michael Nelson just as he was. It was a waste of time to try to conjure up a dream man from the past. Michael had a right to change over the years. Juliet decided to make an effort to get to know and love the man who was her husband now.

She parked the car and opened the trunk to take out their suitcases while the girls ran in ahead of her to find their daddy and tell him all about their trip. Juliet came into the living room with a tote bag in each hand and found Michael in his recliner watching a football game. Daisy was telling him about the ice-skating that they had done that morning. "I only fell down twice, but Mommy never fell down."

"Hi, Michael. Where's Heathcliff?" The dog hadn't greeted Juliet at the garage door, which was totally out of character for him.

"I let him out after church, and he hasn't come back yet," Michael said, continuing to focus on the game.

"What do you mean! You haven't seen him for hours?"

"Juliet, it's no big deal. He'll be back when he sees that you're home."

"I told you to stay with him when he went outside. I'm going to find him." She told the girls to stay with Daddy and ran out the front door.

Juliet race-walked up Pine Avenue as far as Sally's house, calling Heathcliff's name and thinking he might have gone looking for her in that direction. Sally was in her front yard, raking leaves, and said she hadn't seen Heathcliff all day. Juliet walked up and down a few more of the streets they usually took on their frequent walks, and as the minutes passed, her panic grew. By the time she came back to the house and got in her car, she was crying and expecting the worst.

She drove slowly along Conference Drive, looking carefully on both sides of the road. As she left Mount Hermon and turned right on Graham Hill Road, she saw Heathcliff lying on the side of the road, across the street from the grocery store. She quickly pulled over to the shoulder, jumped out of her car, and almost got hit herself as she ran across traffic to reach her precious friend. When she fell to her knees on the ground next to him and saw that there was no hope, Juliet let out a wail.

"Oh, Heathcliff! Oh, no! No!" she shrieked. "Please, please don't leave me." As she hugged him close to her, she realized it was way too late. His poor beautiful body was already stiff with death. She laid her head on his side, sobbing and begging him to forgive her. "I never, never would have left you if I thought this would happen. Oh, Heathcliff, what will I do without you?" She wrapped him in her sweater, lifted him in her arms, and carried him back to the car.

When she parked her car in front of the house, Michael came out and met her in the front yard. He saw instantly that she was crying. "What is it?"

"He's dead." She choked the words out through her tears.

"Juliet, I'm sorry. . . ." He shook his head in disbelief. "I never dreamed anything like this would happen. Heathcliff usually stayed right in the yard."

"Just don't say anything. I can't talk to you right now." Her grief over losing her dearest companion was matched by her fury at Michael for letting her down once again.

"What can I do?"

"Just take the girls out to dinner somewhere so I can be alone and bury him."

Juliet got a shovel from the garage and headed to the wooded area behind their back deck. The ground there was loamy and moist and would be easy to dig. It was already dark, so she turned on the spotlight over the deck to see. She ignored the chill she felt as a cold damp breeze ruffled the hair falling around her face. She went over to the special spot where she had seen Heathcliff go many times to savor a bone, and began to dig.

Juliet was tossing clumps of dirt out of a grave that almost came up to her waist when Sally showed up with a shovel. Juliet looked up at her with tears streaming down her cheeks, and Sally jumped down into the hole and hugged her. "Juliet, I'm so sorry. I called Michael to see if you had found Heathcliff, and he told me you were out here." Juliet laid her head on her friend's shoulder and sobbed.

"What will I do without him?" Juliet wailed pitifully.

"I know how much you loved him. He was such a wonderful dog." Sally choked out the words with tears in her own eyes. "Come on, Juliet, sit down for a while and let me dig."

Juliet sat on the cold, damp dirt by the side of the grave and watched as Sally widened the hole. She shook her head in despair and cried, "He was always there for me. Even if I had just gone to the grocery store for half an hour, he would meet me at the door when I got home and act as if I had been gone for a week. He filled in all the gaps that Michael left. I'll never have another friend like Heathcliff."

Juliet caught her breath and then continued to pour out her agony. "I don't think I'll ever be able to forgive Michael for not watching Heathcliff like I asked him to. And I can't forgive myself for leaving him. He must have gotten confused and left the yard to try and find me." Her voice caught on a sob as she cried, "Oh, Sally, why did I ever go? How could I have been so careless, so disloyal to such a precious friend?"

"Juliet, you can't think like that. Those thoughts will poison you, and they won't bring Heathcliff back."

The two friends finished digging the grave together, then wrapped Heathcliff's poor broken body in his favorite sleeping mat and Juliet's sweater and laid him to rest. Sally walked Juliet back to the house and insisted on staying with her until Michael and the girls returned. She tried to get her to eat a sandwich, but all Juliet could manage was a cup of tea. They sat quietly together at the kitchen table. Every now and then, Juliet burst into fresh tears and reached for the box of tissues.

When Michael came home, the fury Sally saw in Juliet's eyes alarmed her. It was the closest thing to hate Sally had ever seen on her friend's face, and it was directed at Michael. Michael hugged Sally and thanked her for her support as Juliet went upstairs to talk to her daughters. Then he asked in a troubled voice, "Sally, do you think she'll be all right? I don't know what to say or do."

"You know how she adored him, Michael. It's just going to take time for her to adjust."

"I know she's mad at me. She must think it's my fault. I never thought he'd get hit by a car."

"I know. Just be patient. Give her time to absorb the shock." Sally tried to reassure Michael with a confidence in her voice that she didn't feel. She knew she would be praying for the healing of this couple's marriage for a long time to come.

Juliet stayed with the girls in their room that night, and they all cried themselves to sleep. They knew their home would not be the same without their faithful friend.

Chapter Ten

Juliet did not have the luxury of completely giving in to her grief. There was so much to do to get ready for the holidays and her mother-in-law's visit. Busy with shopping, wrapping, baking, and decorating, Juliet went through the motions, but her heart and mind were far away.

Ever since that terrible afternoon when she'd found Michael casually watching a football game while her beloved dog lay dying on the side of the road, Juliet struggled to even speak to her husband. All the years of frustration and disappointment had exploded in her heart on that horrible day and left her completely numb toward Michael. Ironically, her problem of wanting a better love life had been solved in an instant. Now she couldn't bear his casual hugs and infrequent kisses. But she knew she had to keep up appearances–they had two little girls watching them. It would be even harder when Leah arrived.

Within the first day of Leah's visit, the older woman realized her son and daughter-in-law were in trouble. Two nights after her arrival, as she helped Juliet prepare dinner for the girls before Michael and Juliet left for the annual Redwood Real Estate Christmas banquet, Leah asked her daughter-in-law if she wanted to talk.

"Mom, I'm sorry your visit had to be during such a depressing time. I don't mean to spoil everyone's Christmas, but with Heathcliff gone, my heart's just not in it."

"Honey, I understand. I know what a dear friend he was to you. If it weren't for the girls, you'd probably rather skip the holidays this year."

Juliet nodded, her eyes brimming with tears.

"What worries me even more, I'm afraid, are you and Michael," Leah continued. "You've hardly spoken two words to each other since I've arrived. What's happening?"

"He was taking care of Heathcliff for me when Heathcliff wandered off and got hit by the car. I'm having a very hard time dealing with that."

Leah could sense her daughter-in-law's suppressed anger. "Juliet, you don't think Michael intentionally let him get killed, do you?"

"No. It was just the straw that broke the camel's back, as my mom would have said. Remember years ago, what you said about Michael and his dad both being workaholics? That's been really hard on our marriage, too."

"What can you do about it?" Leah was troubled by what she was hearing.

"I've done everything I can over the years, Mom. It's up to Michael now."

A little later, Leah sent her son and his wife off for their party with a request that they not worry about coming home early. She planned to watch some children's holiday specials on television with her granddaughters, and she wanted Michael and Juliet to have some time alone to mend bridges. They made a beautiful couple, with Juliet in a burgundy velvet dress and Michael in a charcoal gray suit and red tie.

Michael tried to talk to Juliet as they drove to the Boulder Creek Country Club, but she answered all his attempts with monosyllables. Aloof and detached, she sat close to the passenger door of the car, looking out the window at the decorated houses lit up with holiday lights in the darkness. Michael was struck by how beautiful she was. He felt as if he had been away on an extended business trip and was seeing her again for the first time in a very long time. He realized once more how thoroughly the stresses of his work and his unpaid bills had been absorbing his time and energy and thoughts.

Juliet's hair was pulled back into a plain, almost severe bun, and there wasn't a trace of a smile on her face. You would think that they were on their way to a funeral instead of to a Christmas party. Her flawless complexion was pale, almost like marble. She looked like an untouchable porcelain queen, and suddenly he realized how desirable she was to him. The sense of longing he felt for Juliet as he turned to admire her at a stop sign shocked him. He couldn't remember when he had last felt such an overpowering need to pull her into his arms and love her. "Juliet." He whispered her name.

She turned and looked at him with her incredible blue eyes, full of unspeakable sorrow and disdain. He realized he had not been forgiven.

As Juliet turned from the buffet with her plate of sole almondine and salad and looked for an empty spot at the banquet tables, she was pleased to find two vacant seats near Michael's secretary. Betty was a plump, middle-aged divorcée with graying hair and a sweet face. She was the devoted mother of three grown children and had many grandchildren. On the few occasions that Juliet had talked with Betty, she had always enjoyed exchanging child-raising stories and ideas.

Juliet was relieved to think that she wouldn't have to make boring small talk with someone she hardly knew and had little in common with. She didn't feel up to introducing herself to newcomers at the office. She was perfectly content to stay in her spot next to Betty all evening, hearing about some Christmas surprises the doting grandmother was planning for her grandchildren.

As the party began to break up and people put on their coats to leave, a new real estate agent, whom Juliet had never met, came over and asked Michael to introduce him. "That's right, you've never met my beautiful bride. Larry, I'd like you to meet the lovely Juliet Nelson."

Larry, a real flirt and ladies' man, openly admired Juliet and kissed her hand while Michael beamed with pride, his arm casually draped around his wife's shoulders.

On the drive home that evening, Juliet let Michael know how disgusted she was with his behavior. "Michael, how can you be such a hypocrite? You've hardly given me a moment's thought in years, and now suddenly, because some womanizer notices me, you act like we have this great marriage."

"I don't know what you're talking about. I've always thought that you're beautiful, and I do think we have a great marriage. Juliet, you've got to stop being mad at me about Heathcliff. I'm really sorry. I wish I could go back and make things right for you."

"This is not about Heathcliff, Michael. This is about us. About the way you completely ignore me until we're in public and you want to look good. I'm not going to play these stupid games with you anymore. I'm not going to be one way in public and another way at home."

"Well, I am sorry that my compliments to you are so offensive. I'll try to control myself in the future." His icy voice told Juliet how exasperated her husband was, but she refused to feel guilty.

Leah's heart sank when Michael and Juliet returned a little after ten o'clock. She had been hoping that they would repair their damaged relationship during their evening together, but if anything, they seemed more out of sorts as they came into the living room where Leah was watching the news. Michael said a quick good night and went upstairs to bed. Juliet followed him but returned a few minutes later, dressed in her nightgown and robe, and sat down next to her mother-in-law on the sofa.

"How were the girls? Did they go to bed okay for you?"

"They were wonderful, as always. I'm wondering about you and Michael. Did the night out give you a chance to talk?"

"We talked a little."

"Do you feel like you were able to work through your problems?"

"Mom, I'm afraid our problems aren't simple enough to be solved with an evening away from the girls. You're just going to have to pray for us."

"Do you think Michael would talk to your pastor with you?"

"It would have to be his initiative. Mom, forgive me if I sound like I don't care about my marriage. I do care. I'm just too discouraged to work on it by myself anymore. Michael has to care, too."

Juliet went up to bed shortly after that, and as Leah sat alone in the beautifully decorated living room, she thought of how much her son would lose if his marriage failed.

She had never known a more loving wife or devoted mother than Juliet. She remembered her frustrations with Steve and how hard it had been to be the wife of a workaholic, and she felt compassion for her daughter-in-law. But as she thought of her two precious granddaughters and the lovely home they had, she prayed that somehow Michael and Juliet would find a way to make peace with one another.

Two nights later, Leah, Juliet, and Michael sat near the front of the sanctuary of Seaside Bible Church to watch Heather and Daisy sing Christmas carols with the children's choir. Lighted candles and a glowing Christmas tree cast a warm light on the two little sisters, who looked like Christmas china dolls in their matching red velvet dresses and hair bows. Juliet's eyes filled with tears as she listened to her daughters singing "Tell Me the Story of Jesus." Their faces were so sweet and sincere, and as Juliet watched them, she wondered how long they would be able to keep that childish innocence. How long before they would have their hearts broken, and their dreams shattered. She longed to gather them into her arms and keep them safe and untouched by the disappointments of life forever.

When Juliet had told them about Heathcliff's death, the girls had been very sad, but not devastated. As she had always suspected, Heathcliff had been her dog.

Michael and the children had enjoyed him, but Juliet was the only family member whose heart had completely bonded with the little dog's heart. Now she thought it was a blessing that the children hadn't become more attached to the dog. They wouldn't be too heartbroken to enjoy the holidays. Unfortunately, Juliet knew that sooner or later something would break their hearts. She was beginning to realize that this was one of the major reoccurring experiences of life.

Early the next morning, Heather crawled into bed next to Juliet and whispered, "Merry Christmas, Mommy." Juliet hugged her and tried to talk her into going back to sleep a little longer, but it was no use. There was no way the little girl could fall back asleep when she had already sneaked downstairs and seen the big pile of presents under the tree. Juliet quietly got out of bed and went with her to the kitchen. They put cinnamon rolls in the oven together and waited for everyone else to wake up.

Michael gave Juliet a new Kathy Smith exercise video that she had mentioned she wanted and a pair of suede moccasins. It wasn't typical of the sentimental and elaborate Christmas gifts he had gotten for her in the past, but Juliet didn't care. It had been so hard for her to finish her holiday shopping after the weekend in San Francisco with her girls. To be fair to Michael, he probably hadn't been in much of a festive mood either. Daisy and Heather were thrilled with the things that they found under the tree, and that was all that mattered to Juliet.

The house got noisy when Jessica, Dan, and their three children arrived that afternoon. As the Nelsons and the Parkers exchanged gifts in the living room, the phone rang. It was Leonard, calling from England and assuring his daughters that he had enjoyed a pleasant Christmas. Jessica came back to the living room after hanging up the phone and commented, "Julie, do you realize this is the first year in our entire lives that we haven't celebrated Christmas and Thanksgiving with Dad?"

"It feels strange, doesn't it? But just think, he's fulfilling a lifelong dream by spending a whole year studying Shakespeare. I'm glad that family he met at church adopted him for Christmas Day. He sounded happy, don't you think?"

Juliet was thankful to have Leah's and Jessica's help with the Christmas cooking. The menu included a beef rib roast and Yorkshire pudding in honor of her dad being in England, and she had never made those dishes before. While Juliet stirred the beef gravy and Jessica prepared a salad, Jessica asked her sister how she was doing. They hadn't seen each other since before Heathcliff died.

"Thanks for asking, Jessie. It helps to keep busy. I know from living through Mom's death that nothing heals as well as time."

"You're right. I guess Michael must be pretty broken up about the whole thing, too," Jessica said.

"I don't know. You'd have to ask him. But he seems fine to me."

"Julie, you're angry with him, aren't you?"

"He seems to know the most efficient ways of breaking my heart. It's downright amazing."

As Michael and Juliet lay in their bed that night, he said softly to her, "Thank you for all you did today, Juliet. It was a really nice Christmas."

"I'm glad you appreciated it." Her voice was muffled.

Michael reached for her hand, but Juliet pulled it away and turned on her side with her back to him. It was hard to believe that a month ago she would have given anything to have him reach out to her. Now she felt frozen inside and repulsed by his touch. She wondered what it would take, or if it was even possible, to melt her heart again.

Chapter Eleven

Juliet was truly relieved to put the holiday decorations away and hang up a new calendar. The morning after New Year's Day, she and the girls took Leah to the airport in San Jose for her flight back to New York. It was going to be hard to say good-bye to this dear woman, who felt like a real mother to her. Having her at their home for the past two weeks had been so comforting and had made the tension of living with Michael easier to bear.

Leah was clearly emotional about leaving as well. Tears were in her eyes as the ticket agent told everyone to line up at the gate to board the plane. She hugged her grandchildren and then turned to her daughter-in-law with an encouraging vote of confidence. "Juliet, I know you and Michael are struggling right now. But I believe that God will give you the wisdom and the ability to make things right again. Please don't give up."

Juliet hugged her tightly, as if trying to gain strength from this wise lady, whom she admired so much. "Thank you for your love and prayers, Mom. You know how much we need them."

As Leah walked down the ramp to board the plane, she called over her shoulder, "Remember, I'm just a phone call away. I love you."

A week later, Juliet and Michael's twelfth wedding anniversary arrived, and she wished that they could just call it off that year. She didn't feel like celebrating with Michael. They didn't have much to say to each other anymore, and the thought of going out to eat with him repelled her. It seemed like a waste of time and money to hire a babysitter and spend hours at a restaurant with someone she didn't want to talk to. And it seemed hypocritical to celebrate a marriage that obviously wasn't working. She decided to ignore the day and see what Michael would do.

That afternoon, Michael called from his office to tell her he had some clients visiting from Minnesota. They only had a few days to find a house before the husband's new job began, and Michael wanted to take them out for a working dinner. Juliet was only too happy to let him off the hook. She ordered pizza to be delivered to the house for her and the girls. They went to bed before Michael came home, and he had already left for work when Juliet got up the next morning.

When she came into the kitchen, she found a vase filled with pink roses on the table and a card from Michael. He wrote, "In spite of all that's happened, I hope you know that I still love you. Always, Michael." A few months before, that note and the pretty flowers would have given her reason to hope. Now, they simply intensified her sorrow. It was too little, too late. She didn't know if there was any way out of the emotional void she was in, and she just didn't care.

When Juliet arrived at the exercise studio later that day, the bulletin board had a new notice about the annual Dancercise convention that would be held at the end of the month in Carmel. She had missed the convention the year before and definitely wanted to make it to this one. Then she would have a chance to be taught the new exercise routines in person and wouldn't have to learn them from videos as she had during the past year.

That evening at the dinner table, while she served her family some chicken stir-fry, Juliet asked Michael what he thought about her going to the convention. "I'd be gone from Friday till Sunday about dinnertime. I know that will mess up your Saturday." She fully expected to hear objections from Michael, but he surprised her.

"No, don't worry about my appointments. I can always take Daisy and Heather to your sister's house for a few hours if I need to work. I think you should go. It would be good for you to have a change of scenery."

Three weeks later, Juliet instructed her daughters to go to Sally's house when they got off the bus after school.

She left for Carmel right after her eleven o'clock Dancercise class, with a promise to her students that she'd be back the next week with challenging new dance routines for everyone. Juliet realized as she drove south that she was looking forward to spending a couple days in one of her favorite little seaside towns, with no obligations to anyone but herself. She hadn't told Michael that the convention didn't actually start until Saturday morning. If she had wanted to, she could have left her home very early on Saturday and still been on time, but she thought a whole day in Carmel might be a tonic for her spirit.

Juliet had reserved a single room for herself at La Playa, instead of trying to share with one of the other aerobics instructors. She had heard about these conventions in the past, and it seemed as though they sometimes became crazy, slumber-party-type weekends. Except for going to the classes that would be held all day Saturday and on Sunday morning, she hoped to keep to herself and have a restful, refreshing weekend.

After Juliet had located the hotel and checked into her room, she realized it was time for a late lunch. She found a deli and bought a turkey-and-avocado croissant and a bottle of lime-flavored mineral water to take to the beach to eat. As she walked down the sidewalk of the quaint little town, she remembered the many visits she had made there with Michael in the early years of their marriage. They had enjoyed spending a Saturday browsing through the intriguing shops, looking for antiques or art to decorate their new home. Her heart was full of bittersweet memories as she sat on the beach and looked out at the green-blue water of Carmel Bay.

Halfway through her croissant and wishing she hadn't left her new murder mystery book back at the hotel, Juliet suddenly noticed a long shadow beside her on the sand. Looking up, she gazed into the face of a dark-haired, dark-eyed, olive-skinned man who seemed startled at the sight of her.

"I'm stunned," he said mostly to himself.

"Is something wrong?" Juliet asked, shielding her eyes from the sun.

He stooped down on the sand next to her and replied candidly, "I was making a bet with myself about what color your eyes would be. With such dark hair, I never imagined they'd be sky blue. It's a shocking contrast—really striking. Do you know how beautiful you are here on the beach with your long dark hair caught in the breeze and your eyes the color of the sky?"

"Are you an artist?" Juliet asked suspiciously. This guy had a line a mile long. Next she expected him to ask her to come to his studio and see his sketches.

"No, but I work with many artists. My name is Robert Solano, and I own the Solano Gallery down the street from here. Sometimes I eat my lunch on the beach like you. Do you mind if I join you?"

He seemed safe enough, and with her book back at the room, she really had nothing better to do while she ate. "I'm Juliet. Please, be my guest."

"Are you new here in Carmel? I know many people, but I'm sure I would have remembered your face."

"I'm just here for a convention. I live near Santa Cruz."

"And what a lovely name you have, Juliet. Like the famous Shakespeare play." He seemed transfixed by her appearance and completely ignored the lunch he had brought.

"Yes, my father was teaching the play *Romeo and Juliet* to his college class when I was born. My sister, Jessica, was born while he was teaching *The Merchant of Venice.* My mother used to tease us and say we were lucky that Dad wasn't teaching *Hamlet* when we were born. We could have ended up being named Ophelia or Gertrude." She smiled as her eyes filled with tears at the memory of her mother.

"Well, Juliet certainly suits you. I can picture the Lady Juliet looking just as you do. Actually, the reason I was so captivated by the sight of you on this beach is because we have an oil painting in my gallery of a lady on this same stretch of beach who looks remarkably like you. I felt as though I was looking at a ghost until I saw that your eyes are blue. The woman in the painting has brown eyes."

"I would like to see that picture. I don't think I've ever been to your gallery. Have you owned it for long?"

"I took it over from a couple who retired about nine years ago. Now I consider Carmel my home. I'd never want to live anywhere else."

"It is a magical place," Juliet agreed. "It's as if there's an invisible sign on the turnoff from Highway 1 to Carmel that says, 'Toss all your troubles out the car window before entering this place.'"

"Have you had many troubles, Juliet?"

She widened her eyes at his question. "What?"

"Forgive me, I know that is a bold thing to ask someone I have just met. But you see, as beautiful as you are, I don't think I've ever met anyone who looks so heartbroken. I am troubled by the pain I see in your eyes."

Juliet felt her heart soften at his candid expression of concern. Maybe he was just a sensitive, overly talkative soul after all. Maybe living in a place like Carmel inspired people to be open like this. "My best friend died last month. I'm trying to adjust to life without him." Her eyes brimmed with tears.

"So you are a widow? I noticed your wedding ring."

"No, I was referring to my dog." She smiled through her tears.

"Oh, I'm sorry. I understand. I have two Himalayan cats that I got when I first bought my shop. They are my constant friends. They come to work with me every day and are wonderful companions. All my customers enjoy Mimi and Muriel. On the rare days when I leave the cats at home, I hear many complaints."

"I'd like to meet them. I have a spoiled Persian at home named Sheba."

"Juliet, I'm going to have to get back to the gallery. But I hate to end this conversation. Since you are a visitor here in town, could I please take you to my favorite Italian restaurant for dinner? It's Raffaello's on Mission. Do you know it?"

"Yes, I've passed it a few times on my way to look at

the shops on Ocean Street. But Robert, you see that I am a married woman. I'm not sure it would be such a good idea."

"We will be meeting as two pet-lovers and appreciators of Shakespeare. How's that?" He smiled warmly at her and seemed so kind and harmless that her reservations melted away.

"Well, I haven't made any plans for dinner. What time would you like to meet?"

"Perhaps six o'clock? I close my shop at five, but there's always so much to attend to before I can leave."

"That sounds nice. I'll meet you at Raffaello's. And thank you. I haven't had Italian food in ages." She was warming up to the idea.

Back at her hotel, Juliet kept debating with herself about whether or not she was making a huge mistake. She stretched out on the bed and tried to distract herself with the mystery novel, but her mind kept going back to the interesting man she had just met. Robert was undeniably attractive with his black hair, deep-brown eyes, and a beautiful smile that made his eyes dance. She decided that it would be safe to meet him for dinner if she set some guidelines for herself before she left the hotel room. She knew how vulnerable she was to the attentions of a handsome man after all the neglect she had endured from Michael.

Juliet soaked in a bubble bath for almost an hour and then dressed in a simple, black wool shift and black angora cardigan. She pulled her freshly washed hair back into a French knot, then took it back out, deciding that she liked it better falling straight down her back. She pushed the front of her hair back with a black velvet headband, allowing only a shadow of bangs to brush across her forehead. As she fastened the clasp on her cameo necklace, she pretended to be her older sister, Jessica, lecturing the younger Juliet before a high school date.

"Okay, here are the rules. Have as much fun flirting and feeling like a real woman again as you like, but when dinner is over, you will come right back here and sleep in this hotel bed by yourself." She smiled to herself and wondered how long it had been since the thought of eating dinner out with a man had made her heart race.

She was a little late and slightly out of breath when she reached Raffaello's and was pleasantly surprised to see Robert standing on the sidewalk in front of the restaurant, waiting for her. The expression on his face made her blush and told her that she had chosen the right thing to wear.

"It is hard to believe that you are even more beautiful at this moment than you were on the beach earlier today." He was practically drooling.

"Thank you. I don't know what to say." She hadn't felt this flustered since she was sixteen years old.

"Say nothing, Juliet. Just gazing at you is a feast for my soul. What a privilege it will be to look at you across the dinner table."

"Well, shall we go inside then?" His piercing gaze was making her feel faint, and she desperately wanted to talk about something other than how she looked.

When they got inside, she discovered that he had already

reserved his favorite table in the corner by the window, and a bottle of white wine sat chilling next to a platter of antipasto. As she sipped some wine and nibbled on some marinated vegetables, she found herself melting under the admiration of this delightful man. Everyone at the restaurant seemed to know and love Robert. And they all wanted to meet his lovely companion. Finally, everyone seemed to get the message that he wanted to be left alone with his lady friend, and they were able to continue their conversation from earlier on the beach.

"You know, Robert, I have to tell you the truth. I must have talked myself out of coming here tonight three times before I actually left the hotel to meet you."

"I was afraid you might change your mind. That is why I was waiting for you outside the restaurant. I was going to run after you if you started to turn around."

"I've never done anything like this in twelve years of marriage." She sighed and reached for her glass of wine.

"I'm honored. What made you have dinner with me then?"

She decided to be totally honest with him. After all, she'd probably never see him again, and he might be able to help her understand what was wrong with her marriage. A man's point of view seemed very valuable at the moment. "Robert, you must realize how charismatic you are. And I can spot a genuine pet-lover a mile away. But I have a very selfish reason for being here. I'm in trouble right now in my marriage, and I was hoping that maybe you could help me figure out what's gone wrong. Have you ever been married?"

"Oh, yes. Shortly after I took over the gallery, I met and married a young artist whose work I greatly admired. She specialized in sunsets, and I was sure that anyone who could paint a sunset so beautifully must have a soul that I could relate to. I was wrong."

"What happened?"

"She was a free spirit. One day I came home early from work and found her in our bed with a jewelry maker who worked in a shop down the street from mine."

"What a nightmare."

"She moved out soon after that. The last I heard of her, she was living with another artist in Santa Fe."

"I'm sorry, Robert," she said quietly.

"This all happened years ago. I'm over it now. Sadder, but wiser."

"I guess I was right in thinking that you might be someone who could give me a man's perspective of marriage. What do you suppose makes a man lose interest in his wife over the years?"

"I can't understand any man who would lose interest in you, Juliet. You are so lovely. I guess if a woman stops caring about her appearance or stops being a lover to her man after the marriage . . . that would be very damaging."

"What about a husband who stops wanting to be a lover to his wife after years of marriage? Do you know what could make that happen?"

"Please don't tell me this is your problem. Any man who was married to you and stopped wanting to make love to you would have to be either dead or insane."

Juliet burst out laughing at his indignant remark. "Oh, thank you, Robert! I wish I'd met you years ago."

"So do I."

"Seriously though, are there things that happen to a man after marriage? Things that press in on him and cause him to lose touch with the passion that started the relationship in the first place?"

"Well, I can only speak from the experience I had with my brief marriage to Annabelle. I married her at the same time that I was taking over the ownership of my art gallery. It was a very stressful time. I never stopped being attracted to her, but she may have felt neglected at times because of the long hours I was working. She was young and couldn't see past the temporary pressure we were under. Also, I've wondered since our divorce if I rushed into marriage too quickly. Annabelle and I had very different philosophies of marriage. I was raised to think of marriage as a sacred, lifelong commitment, but she seemed to have a casual attitude about the whole thing."

"Yes, I think our parents play a big part in how we think about marriage. My parents always had a passionate relationship. It made a lasting impression on me."

They enjoyed a delightful dinner together. Juliet told him about her little girls and the Dancercise convention, and Robert described how his family had moved to America from Naples, Italy, when he was a teenager. By the time they finished their cappuccinos, Juliet felt as if she'd known Robert for years. He was so easy to talk to and seemed to understand the issues of her heart in a way no other man ever had.

Robert asked Juliet to walk over to his art gallery after dinner to see the painting of the woman he had told her about. As they left the restaurant, it seemed completely natural for Juliet to put her hand through the bent arm that Robert held out to her. She was feeling a little unsteady. Though she rarely drank any alcohol, she had sipped a little more than two glasses of wine with her dinner. Robert had ordered a bottle of his favorite Chardonnay for her, and she hadn't wanted to hurt his feelings by refusing to drink any. She hoped the walk to his art studio in the fresh salt air would bring her back to her senses.

The Solano Gallery was only a few blocks away from Raffaello's, and Juliet was enchanted with its beautiful atmosphere. The walls were painted a very pale sky blue and lightly touched with white on the ceilings to give a subtle hint of clouds. The concrete floors were textured with sand in a way that made them look and feel like the beach. Several gallery rooms featured lovely paintings by local artists, and in the back were a sitting room and office.

Robert led Juliet right away to the room on their left where the painting of her "twin," as he referred to her, was hanging. As Juliet studied the painting, she understood his surprise at finding her on the beach that afternoon. Even the heather-blue sweater and jeans the woman in the portrait was wearing were similar to the ones Juliet had worn that day.

"You weren't exaggerating, Robert. I wonder if I was a twin?"

"They say that everyone on the earth has a twin brother or sister somewhere."

"Do you know this artist or the woman he painted?" The more she studied the painting, the more intrigued she became.

"No. I bought this at an auction in San Jose last year."

"I was born in San Jose."

"Well, the plot thickens. Perhaps she is a long-lost cousin. Can I pour you an amaretto or some sherry?" He took her hand and led her to a beige leather sofa in his office. Juliet sank down onto the comfortable cushions, feeling a little dizzy.

"Could I just have a glass of water, please? I'm afraid I won't be able to walk back to my hotel if I drink any more alcohol."

"I must tell you, Juliet. That's what I was hoping for." He sat down next to her on the sofa and sipped his sherry as he studied the cameo necklace she was wearing. "This necklace looks like the ones my uncle makes in his factory in Italy."

"It was purchased in Italy a very long time ago. This is an heirloom I got on my wedding day." She looked up from the necklace to meet Robert's eyes. He was no longer studying the necklace but instead was looking intently into her eyes. She didn't resist when his finger traced a gentle path from her eyebrow to her lips. He pulled her into his arms and kissed her, tentatively, and then insistently. She returned his kisses with all the passion and desire she had bottled up for years. Then she remembered that she wasn't kissing Michael. She pushed him away and began to cry.

"Robert, this is all wrong. I'm married. I can't do this."

"Juliet, my house is not far from here. Please come and spend the night with me." He smoothed back her hair and kissed her neck and shoulders, and Juliet would have loved nothing more than to shut out the screaming warnings in her mind and agree to go with him. Robert gently pushed her down on the sofa and softly said, "You are so beautiful, Juliet. I want to show you how desirable you are." She melted under one more incredible kiss and then wriggled out from under him and quickly stood up next to the sofa. She was breathless and trembling.

"I'm sorry, Robert. Thank you for wanting me, but this is just all wrong."

"Juliet, I promise you won't regret it. Come home with me." He stretched his hand out to her, but she refused to take it.

"No, Robert. If I go with you, I'll hate myself for doing something we both know is wrong. I have to go now." She grabbed her purse and almost ran out of the gallery and into the street, terrified that if she stayed any longer, he would convince her to change her mind.

Back in the safety of her hotel room, Juliet stood in the shower, crying and trying to wash away the feeling of being dirty. She knew that she had been playing with fire to go out with such an attractive man at such a low point in her marriage. What had surprised her was the loyalty she still felt for Michael in spite of his repeated rejection of her over the years.

She tossed and turned for most of the night and dragged herself out of bed the next morning to get some coffee at La Playa's Terrace Grill before the long day of Dancercise lessons began. As she walked into the restaurant, she was shocked to see Robert sitting at a table and watching people enter through the doorway. He jumped up from his seat as Juliet came into the room, hurried over to her, and asked her to please join him. She sat down in the chair he pulled out for her, and saw that he had put a single, long-stemmed red rose on her plate. The perfect bud was delightfully fragrant and just beginning to open.

"Robert, this is such a sweet surprise. I thought you'd be angry with me for leaving so suddenly last night."

"Juliet, I am far from angry. I want to thank you for restoring my faith in women. When my wife was unfaithful to me all those years ago, I thought that perhaps all women were like Annabelle. I've met very few women in the years since my divorce who gave me a reason to form any other opinion. Your determination to be loyal to your husband last night in spite of the problems in your marriage impressed me greatly. He is a lucky man to have such a wife."

Tears filled Juliet's eyes, and at first she couldn't speak because of the big knot that had formed in her throat. "I'm sorry I painted such a negative picture of my husband last night. He really has many wonderful qualities. We're just going through such a difficult time."

"I know, but I want to encourage you that most marriages I know that have lasted also have gone through deep valleys, just as you are experiencing right now. Juliet, if for some reason you and Michael don't make it through your valley, will you come back here and let me know? I want the best for you, but if your husband is too foolish to try to save his marriage to such an incredible woman, I want to be the first in line to take his place."

She blushed and said with an embarrassed smile, "Robert, you have showered me with far more compliments than I deserve. The woman who marries you someday surely will be blessed. You are a very dear man. Just make sure she's willing to make a wholehearted commitment to you."

"Believe me, I've learned that lesson."

They drank some coffee and ate croissants with strawberry jam, and then Juliet saw the time and regretfully told him that she had to go. He kissed her on the cheek as he left her at the meeting room where the Dancercise group was gathering, and she wondered if she would ever see him again. It was a happy ending to a situation that could have been very ugly.

Her emotions in turmoil, Juliet thought about the events of the past day. It had been wrong to go so far with Robert the night before. To drink to the point of letting down her guard had been foolish. She deeply regretted having even met Robert for dinner, the first step on the slippery slope, and wondered how she would tell Michael that she had compromised her vows.

As she struggled through it all in her mind, Juliet began

to realize that when she said no to Robert last night she was saying yes to Michael and her marriage. She had been mourning her dying marriage, much as she had been mourning Heathcliff's death, but Juliet realized that her marriage wasn't yet dead. It had cooled, but wasn't ready for the grave. Perhaps there was hope.

Something had shifted in Juliet in the past twenty-four hours. She was no longer willing to stand by and simply watch her marriage crumble and die. She was determined it would be as good as or better than it had ever been. Nothing else would do.

Chapter Twelve

When Juliet came home late that Sunday afternoon, Michael sensed that something was different about her. She seemed energized and confident, and the lost look had left her eyes. She set her suitcase down in the living room, and Daisy and Heather ran to greet her.

"Mommy, Mommy, I missed you!" Heather hugged Juliet as she knelt on the floor.

"I missed you, too. Wait till you see the new dances I have to teach you." The girls enjoyed learning the dance routines with their mom before she taught them to her paying students.

Daisy announced in a grown-up voice that she and her daddy had fixed dinner themselves. Juliet looked over at Michael with a surprised expression. She had never known him to volunteer to cook anything. Daisy grabbed her mom's hand and pulled her out to the kitchen to show her the canned beef stew that was simmering in a pot on top of the stove.

"See, Mommy. This is the kind of stew we had at Aunt Jessica's house, and Daddy and I made some for you!"

"That's great, Daisy. I really didn't want to have to cook tonight."

"Yeah. And we're having ice-cream cake for dessert."

"My, what's the big occasion?"

"You're home!"

Juliet's heart ached as she realized she had some painful announcements to make before the night was over.

After they had eaten and the girls had been put to bed, Juliet asked Michael to sit and talk with her in the living room. She had done a lot of thinking since her evening with Robert, and she felt that there was only one thing to do. She sat down on the sofa and took a deep breath. "Michael, I need to tell you about something that happened this weekend."

"It must have been good. You look almost like your old self again."

"Actually, what happened was that I almost went home with a man I'd just met."

"What! What did he do to you?"

"He invited me out to dinner, and we had a wonderful conversation. Then he took me to his art gallery and kissed me and made me feel beautiful and desirable. Even I didn't realize how starved I was for attention until a total stranger took an interest in me."

"And you allowed this total stranger to kiss you? Is that all he did?" Michael looked furious.

"I promise you that all I did was kiss him. But it makes

my head spin to think how close I came to going home with him. We are in trouble, Michael. I've told you this before. Maybe now you'll agree with me."

"I can't believe you'd do something like this," Michael said incredulously as he shook his head.

"I can't believe I'd stand by and watch a beautiful marriage fall apart at the seams. I think you should move out for a while, Michael." Juliet felt stronger and more determined with every word she spoke.

"What are you saying? Do you want a divorce?" Looks of anger and hurt flashed across his face, and he looked at Juliet as if he didn't know her.

"No, I don't want a divorce. I just don't think that we're going to be motivated to take our marriage problems seriously as long as we're living under the same roof. We need some time away from each other to figure out how we've gotten to such an unhealthy place and how we can get out of it."

"Maybe we should talk to a marriage counselor, but I don't see any reason to cause some big scandal and have all our friends talking about us. You know that's what will happen if I move out."

"I can't think anymore about what Sally and John will say, or what our friends at church will think. I am dying inside, and I need to do something drastic to save this marriage before it's too late. So what if we blow everyone's illusion of us as the perfect family? It's not the truth anyway. I am not willing to live a lie any longer. I need a real husband, Michael. A real lover."

Michael got up from the sofa, turned his back on his

wife, and went upstairs to put some clothes in a suitcase. Juliet followed him to their bedroom and sat quietly on the white love seat, petting Sheba and wondering if she was making the biggest mistake in her life. Her voice sounded very small as she asked him, "Where will you go?"

"Do you care?" Michael answered sarcastically. But when he turned, he saw tears running down her cheeks. "I guess I'll see if Bill will let me use his guest room for a while." His former college roommate had gotten divorced five years before and was living in a condominium in Capitola. "What will you tell Daisy and Heather?" His voice choked with emotion.

"I'll tell them the truth. That we have a problem with our marriage and that we need to get some help to fix it."

Tears filled both of their eyes as he gave her one long, last look and walked down the stairs and out to the garage. Juliet heard the car start and the garage door open and close. In the quiet of her bedroom, she began to grieve—for all the broken dreams, for all the disappointments, for all the beautiful memories that now only brought her pain. She felt as if someone had died. And that someone was herself.

She stared into the cold fireplace and talked to God about what she had done. "Please forgive me for what I did this weekend. I know it was a sin to go with Robert, and I have no excuse for myself. Oh, Father, I want Michael back. Not the man he's become, but the Michael he used to be. Is it too late? Have I ruined everything? Please, please help us. We are in so much trouble." She laid her head down on the love seat next to Sheba and cried until she was too weak to cry anymore. She was terrified that she had pushed Michael away for good. What if he never forgave her? What if he gave up and asked for a divorce? She stood up and went downstairs to fix some tea.

As she sat at the kitchen table, drinking peppermint tea and reviewing the past few years of her marriage, she realized that what she had done was painful but necessary. Her marriage had been dying a slow but certain death. She had made things more complicated by going out with Robert, but the marriage had been in serious trouble for months. And if she hadn't made Michael leave, he would have used his hectic work schedule as an excuse not to work on their problems. No matter how painful it was or how much she wanted to call Bill's house and check on Michael, she would force herself to wait until he made the next move.

The girls didn't notice their daddy was gone until the next night at dinner. Daisy was curious when her mom told her to put only three plates on the table for dinner. "Where's Daddy? Does he have to work tonight?"

"No, sweetheart. I guess I should talk to both of you right now. Heather, can you come here? I need to tell you something. Daddy is staying with Uncle Bill for a while."

"What? Daddy is staying with Uncle Bill? Why would he do that?" Heather seemed confused.

"Daddy and I are having some problems in our marriage, and we thought we could fix them better if we lived in different houses for a while."

"Are you going to get a divorce?" Daisy asked with a frightened look on her face. "My friend Tracy, from school, just moved to an apartment in Brookdale because her parents got a divorce and her mom couldn't afford their big house."

"No, Daisy. I don't want to get a divorce. You know how I make you and Heather have a time-out in different rooms sometimes when you're fighting? Sometimes when we're disagreeing with someone, it's easier to work it out if we're apart for a while."

"So you're making Daddy take a time-out?" Heather struggled to make sense of the situation. The look on her little face was so puzzled and innocent, Juliet just had to pull the child onto her lap and hug her.

"Yes. Daddy and I are both having a time-out." She pulled Daisy over to join in their hug, and tried to speak confidently, wanting to believe what she told her daughters. "I'm sure we'll work it all out soon. Just remember that Daddy and I love you both more than anything in the whole world."

The three of them hugged one another. Then Juliet pulled away and looked at the girls closely. "How do you feel about all this? Are you okay?"

Daisy responded first. "As long as you don't get a divorce, I guess it's okay."

Heather asked, "When will we see Daddy again?"

When Juliet assured the girls that their dad would be coming by to see them soon, they both said they felt all right about the situation. But after Juliet said their bedtime prayers with them, the girls wanted her to stay and sleep in their room. She was happy to agree. The night before had been miserable. Several times she had rolled over in her sleep and realized that Michael wasn't there. She had started to cry and then dozed back off into a fitful sleep. It would be comforting to cuddle next to her sweet little girls.

Juliet finally got a call from Michael on Tuesday night while she was fixing dinner. Daisy answered the phone and told her father in a very mature tone of voice that she knew all about his and Mommy's time-out. After she let Heather say hello, they handed the phone to Juliet.

"Hi. How's it going?" Juliet tried to sound casual.

"Bill's guest room is pretty comfortable, but his cooking could use some improvement."

"He's willing to let you stay for a while?"

"Yes, but I don't want to stay. Juliet, do you think you could hire a sitter and meet me for dinner tomorrow night? We need to talk. In fact, why don't you take the girls to Jessica's house, so if we're too late, she can keep them for the night."

"I haven't told Jessie anything yet. I haven't talked to anyone but the girls about what's going on."

"Well, go ahead and tell Jessica. It's going to get out sooner or later anyway."

Juliet agreed to meet him the next night at Chaminade. Then she called her sister and had a painful conversation with her, telling her about the state of her marriage. Jessica was more than happy to have her nieces come for the evening. She promised Juliet that she would be praying for her marriage.

Juliet took longer than usual to prepare for her meeting with Michael. She felt that in order to have the confidence she needed to hold her ground with her husband, she had to know that she looked her best. The next afternoon, before she took the girls to Jessica's, she spent hours grooming and carefully choosing the perfect outfit. She finally decided on a navy blue cashmere sweater and a long, flowered skirt. Her hair was held back with a navy velvet headband, and she wore a sapphire necklace that Michael had given her years before.

She parked her car near the entrance of Chaminade and slowly walked toward the lobby doors, taking deep breaths of the salty evening air. Michael stood inside the doorway, and Juliet was relieved to see him smile. They didn't say anything to each other as he reached for her hand and led her back out the front door. He explained what he was planning as they walked down the pathway to the room that had been their honeymoon suite more than twelve years before. "I knew we'd want a lot of privacy to talk tonight, so I had our dinner brought to the room."

As he opened the door, Juliet was bombarded with memories of the last time she had been in that room. Michael tipped the waiter, who was finishing the setup of their dinner table. He had ordered steaks, baked potatoes, and salads for both of them. After assuring the waiter that they wouldn't need anything else and closing the door, Michael went to stand next to Juliet at the window. A tear traced a path down her cheek as she stood, lost in thought, looking out into the darkness.

"Juliet." He whispered her name as he tentatively took her into his arms. She didn't say anything as he gently undressed her and pulled her into bed with him. Afterward, Juliet lay next to him, completely surprised by the way the evening was turning out. She wouldn't deny that it was wonderful to make love with Michael again, but they had hardly said a word to each other. She realized she was hungry, so she put on her slip and went over to the dinner table to see if anything was still good enough to eat. Michael pulled on his pants and sat across the table from her as they ate cold steak and salad and finally started to talk.

"I've missed you, Juliet. The past three nights have been agony."

"I know."

"I want to come home."

"Michael, we haven't fixed anything."

"How can you say that after making love?"

"Look, just because we made love doesn't mean our problems are gone." She knew she had to be strong, even though she would have loved nothing more than to call a truce.

"And what do you think our problems are, Juliet?"

"Well, for one thing, you hardly ever communicate with me. I never know what's going on in your heart or your head. I've been very lonely for the past few years."

"I've been under incredible pressure for a long time now." He'd never planned to talk about it, but he realized he needed to now.

"What kind of pressure, Michael?"

"You know the real estate market has been in a slump for the past few years. I haven't been making the volume of sales that I used to make. I've had a hard time keeping up with our bills. I've taken out some extra loans on the house. We've come close to foreclosure a couple of times in the past four years or so."

She felt as if she had been kicked in the stomach. "Why didn't you tell me any of this before?"

"I didn't want you to worry," he answered quietly.

"Michael, I feel as betrayed as you must have felt the other night when I told you I'd gone out with another man. Don't you think I have a right to know when we aren't able to pay our bills? I'm your wife."

"Don't try to compare this with your going out with that other guy. I kept our money problems to myself to protect you. That's different than what you did."

"The way I see it, you didn't trust me enough to be

honest with me, so you shut me out. You built a wall around yourself. You were protecting your pride, Michael, not me." She clasped her hands together tightly and looked down at them on her lap. Her entire body began to tremble with rage.

"Maybe that's how you see it, but my motive was to keep from upsetting you with our problems," he said defensively.

"So instead, you upset me more by living in an emotional shell. Why did you think I wouldn't be able to deal with a money problem?"

"I know how much you love living in our house and the comfortable lifestyle we have."

"Let's get one thing straight, Michael Nelson. I was the kid from the townhouse in San Jose, and you were the rich real estate agent with the BMW when we met. Remember? It's always been your goal to have a lot of money, not mine. I just wanted you." As she said this, her voice broke and she stood up to pull on her sweater and skirt.

"What are you doing?"

"I'm going home."

"I'll come, too." He stood up from the table and began to put on his shirt.

"No, Michael. We need to work through these problems before we live together again. You think it's reasonable to keep secrets from me, and I'm feeling like I've been married to a stranger for the past few years." She grabbed her purse and hurried out of the room without waiting for him.

She cried all the way home to Mount Hermon, deciding as she passed the Scott's Valley exit to let Jessica keep the girls for the night. It was past their bedtime, and they would know that she had been crying if she went to get them now. She felt like her legs were dragging weights as she climbed up the stairs to her bedroom. The problems she and Michael faced seemed like a huge mountain towering ahead of her. She felt completely drained and numb and incapable of thinking clearly. She stretched out on her bed without even undressing and fell into a deep sleep.

Chapter Thirteen

Juliet woke up to the sound of the phone ringing early the next morning. It was Jessica, offering to take the girls to school and asking Juliet to come over for lunch. When Juliet got to her sister's house a few hours later, she saw that Jessica had set the table with a lovely bouquet of flowers and an attractively presented lunch of chicken salad croissants and fresh fruit salad.

"Jessie, this is so thoughtful. First, you watch my kids, feed them dinner, and take them to school, and now this beautiful lunch. I don't deserve all this."

"Of course you do. Don't you know that I love you, Julie?" At that, Juliet put her face in her hands and began to cry. Jessica walked over and hugged her. Tears filled the older sister's eyes as the two women sat down at the kitchen table. Jessica handed Juliet a tissue and said in her big-sister voice, "Come on now, dry your tears and eat with me."

"Where's Kevin?" Juliet noticed that her three-year-old nephew wasn't anywhere to be seen.

"I took him to the baby-sitter's house today. I wanted to be able to talk to you without any distractions. I'm worried about you, kiddo. Do you feel like you solved anything at dinner last night with Michael? I was hoping that you'd kiss and make up and he'd come home with you."

"Jessie, I wish it could be fixed that easily. These problems of ours are bigger than I even realized."

"Is he involved with another woman?"

"No. At least that's not one of our problems."

"Are you going to talk to your pastor or someone else about it?"

"I'm leaving that up to Michael. He's the one who never wants to talk. I think it would be a waste of time for us to meet with the pastor if all Michael was going to do was sit there and let me do the talking. He has to take the initiative to fix this thing. He has to be willing to talk it all out."

"Did he open up at all last night?"

"Sort of. But then I got mad and left."

"Well, it has to work out. I know you love each other, even if you feel like things look hopeless right now. Your girls are going to be disappointed. They were hoping that their daddy was coming home last night."

"I don't want him to move back until things are healthy between us. As long as we're apart, I think he'll be motivated to work on it."

"Julie, remember last fall when I told you about the women's Bible study that was starting after Christmas? I've been going to it for a few weeks now, and it's been wonderful. Our teacher is so wise and challenging. I didn't talk to you about it after Christmas because you were so upset after Heathcliff died. But now I'm going to insist that you come with me at least once. Dan has offered to watch your girls. They meet on Tuesday nights. Please say you'll come."

"Okay. I'll try it once. But I can't promise that I'll go more than that."

"Just come once, and you'll want to keep coming."

When Juliet picked up her girls at school that afternoon, Heather complained that her head hurt and her throat was sore. Juliet took her temperature when they got home. It was 102 degrees. She settled Heather on the sofa with a cold drink and began fixing dinner.

Juliet was sharing a pizza with Daisy a little later when the phone rang. Daisy grabbed it, hoping it would be her dad, and she wasn't disappointed. She talked to him for a while and took the phone to Heather so that she could hear his voice, too. Then he asked to talk to their mommy.

"I'm sorry Heather is sick. What do you think is wrong?"

"It looks like the flu. I've asked one of the other Dancercise instructors to teach my classes for me tomorrow and maybe even next week. If it is the flu, she may be sick for a while."

"Make sure you and Daisy take your vitamins. You don't want to get it, too. When can we get together again?"

"It's going to be complicated with Heather being sick. I don't want anyone to baby-sit for her and end up getting sick themselves. Besides, I just don't want to be away from her when she's like this. She needs me."

"Why don't I come over there and talk?"

"Michael, you've got me all unsettled and confused by the things you said last night. I haven't thought everything through yet. I need some time."

"Juliet, I'm sorry things turned out the way they did last night. I want to get to the bottom of these issues of ours."

"What you need is some soul-searching. You need to understand why you don't want to be honest with me. Maybe we'll have more to talk about when you figure that out. I'm exhausted, Michael. Just give me a few days to process all that's happened, okay?"

Michael felt extremely annoyed as he hung up the phone. He couldn't remember another time in his marriage when he had been so frustrated with his wife. Juliet had always been so loving and agreeable. Now she was demanding and inflexible. And it didn't help matters that Bill was hammering on him every day, asking him when he was going to see Juliet and work things out. As Michael walked out of the kitchen, Bill looked up from watching TV and started badgering him again.

"What did she say? Are you going to get together?"

"No. Heather has the flu, and Juliet doesn't want to leave her with a sitter." Michael sounded as dejected as he felt.

"Mike, Heather is your kid, too. Go over there and give them some moral support. Take some orange juice and chicken soup."

"Juliet doesn't want me there. She says she needs some space to deal with everything that's happened."

"Mike, I'm bugging you about this because you're my oldest and best friend. Juliet is the girl for you. Don't let your marriage go. Believe me, you don't want to get divorced. It's a lousy place to be. If you have to kick the door in and kidnap her till she comes to her senses, do it. Don't let her go."

By the time Saturday arrived, Daisy had a fever, too, and Juliet was running a twenty-four-hour hospital. She fixed up the living-room sofas like beds for the girls during the day so that they could be near the kitchen and watch television. At night, she slept in their room, emptying their pans when they threw up, wiping off their faces with cold washcloths, and refilling their drinks. When Michael called on Saturday night, she was in the kitchen, fixing some tea and toast for Heather.

"Hi! How are my girls?"

"Daisy is sick now, too." Juliet sounded tired and harassed.

"You've got your hands full then. What can I do?"

"Just pray for us. Sally told me yesterday that this thing lasts at least a week. A lot of the kids in school are down with it."

Juliet insisted that she didn't want Michael to come over, but he ignored her and showed up on Sunday afternoon. He came into the living room with the latest Disney video and a big box of Popsicles. The girls squealed with delight at the sight of him. Juliet was quiet. She put the movie into the VCR and started it, gave each of the girls a cherry Popsicle, and took the rest of the package out to the kitchen to put in the freezer. Michael followed her.

"What's wrong, Juliet?"

"I told you I'm not ready to talk to you yet, Michael."

"I miss you. I want to see my kids. Don't I have a right to be here? You're my family."

"Yes. You have a right to see your daughters. They're obviously encouraged to have you here. Please feel free to visit them."

"But I need to talk to you, Juliet. We need to sort out our problems."

"Isn't it ironic? For years I've been pleading with you to work on our marriage with me. Now that I'm busy with two sick girls and hardly have a chance to think straight, you need to talk about the marriage. Well, I'm just not ready."

"I've never known you to be so stubborn, Juliet. Why are you doing this? Let me come home. We'll work on the marriage when you feel like talking. I won't rush you. But I want to be here with all of you. You're my wife. We belong together."

"Why should I trust you? Why should I think you really want to fix what's wrong with us? All you want to do is move back home so you can relax and take me for granted again."

Michael ended the conversation with Juliet because he knew if he didn't he'd begin shouting. He went upstairs to get more clean clothes and took them out to his car. Then he hugged his little girls good-bye, with a promise to call them in a day or so. Juliet was in the laundry room putting clothes in the dryer and didn't come out to see him go.

As he drove back to Bill's condominium, Michael's emotions alternated between rage, grief, and fear. He realized that they were in trouble way over their heads. For a long time, Michael had thought that if only his ability to make love with Juliet would return, their relationship would be good again. Now, for reasons he couldn't understand, he was able and eager to make love with his wife, but that was apparently not enough for her anymore. Now Juliet was insinuating that sharing his body wasn't the only thing she needed from him. She wanted him to share his heart and his soul, too. But when he had been honest with her about their money problems at Chaminade the other night, she'd gotten furious and refused to talk to him.

He knew that he needed to get some advice, so he decided to drive on to Aptos and stop in at his associate pastor's house. He had helped Ron Forsythe and his wife find their house when they had moved to the area two years earlier. They hadn't stayed in touch, except for seeing each other occasionally at church, but Michael was desperate and hoped Ron would be willing to talk with him.

Ron Forsythe looked surprised when he answered the doorbell and found Michael standing on the front porch. He was very gracious and dismissed Michael's apology for showing up without calling first. He led his guest into a book-lined study, off the front hallway, and shut the door. As Michael sat across the desk from him, he felt his tension begin to melt away. Pastor Forsythe was probably about the same age Michael's father would have been, were he still living. He had thinning salt-and-pepper hair and faded gray eyes that seemed to look right into a person's soul, not with judgment but with love and compassion. "It's great to see you again, Michael, but from the look on your face, I think you have a problem."

"Juliet asked me to move out a week ago. I just came from our house, and she doesn't seem to be in any hurry for me to come back."

"I'm sorry. What happened?"

"From what she's told me, Juliet's biggest gripe about our marriage is that she feels like I don't communicate enough with her. Like I shut her out of my life." He wasn't ready to share the fact that she had been dissatisfied with their sex life, too.

"This is one of the biggest issues I counsel husbands and wives about. In marriage counseling, the problem you're describing is about as common as a cold."

Michael was encouraged by that comparison. "Well then, if it's as simple as having a cold, do you think it will be as easy to solve?"

"That will be up to you and Juliet. The fundamental problem seems to be that men tend to be more withdrawn, while most women want to share their feelings. In the best marriages, couples try to give each other what they need, even when they don't necessarily feel like it."

"The problem is, I get buried in the pressures of my job and don't even realize I'm shutting her out. I don't do it intentionally. I love Juliet, but she doesn't feel like I do."

"Have you always been so busy and preoccupied with your work, or is this just a recent problem?"

"For years now, my job has been pretty much six or seven days a week and all-consuming."

"A lot of us in the ministry deal with this issue, too, Michael. It's hard sometimes to ignore the legitimate pressures you face at work and spend a day or a weekend relaxing and reconnecting with your wife and family."

"That's the way it is. If someone wants to look at houses or I have paperwork to catch up on, I don't feel right about ignoring that to goof off. We have a lot of bills to pay."

"The trouble, though, is that if you don't connect with Juliet and the kids, they will become your all-consuming problem. You probably realize this, now that Juliet has asked you to move out. Having problems at home makes it hard, if not impossible, to be productive at your job."

"I know. What can I do, Ron?"

"Are you familiar with the gospel passages where Jesus tells the Pharisees that the reason Moses permitted people to divorce was because of the hardness in their hearts?"

"Now wait—we're not talking at all about divorce. Juliet just asked me to move out for a while."

"Hear me out, Michael. I'm not suggesting that you and Juliet will get a divorce; in fact, I'll be praying earnestly that you don't. What I'm saying is that in my years of counseling I've found that most relationship problems begin with this issue of hardness of heart. Somewhere along the line, feelings are hurt, grudges are built, and husbands and wives begin to harden their hearts against one another."

Michael shook his head and said with a bewildered look, "I don't feel like I have a hard heart toward Juliet."

"But somehow she must not be receiving the love you feel for her; otherwise she wouldn't be so angry with you. It would help me to hear what Juliet's perspective of the problem is. Do you think she would come in for counseling with you?"

"I doubt it. She doesn't want to talk with me or even see me at this point."

"It sounds to me like she's been hurting for a long time and the volcano has erupted. If I were you, I would use this time apart to pray for wisdom to understand your wife. Ask God to show you what you've done to damage your relationship with Juliet, and pray for guidance to know when and how to make the next move. If Juliet says she needs time, show her that you love and respect her by giving her time to sort out her feelings. I would keep making loving gestures while you're apart, though. You could send her cards with short notes in them. And call every day or two to talk to the kids and to her, if she'll let you. Some loving attention and lots of prayer may turn the whole thing around. I'd like to keep meeting with you regularly, Michael. And when Juliet is ready, I'd like to meet with both of you."

"So you don't think it's hopeless?"

Ron smiled sympathetically. "I know it's hard in the middle of a crisis to believe that things will be good again. But you know, even now, while Juliet is refusing to speak to you, there is something powerful you can do to start to heal your marriage."

"You're saying I can fix my marriage even when Juliet isn't speaking to me? How?"

"You need to spend time alone with God. Let's be realistic. The only thing in life you have any real control over is yourself. There are always two sides to a marriage problem. When I meet with husbands and wives, usually they both have legitimate reasons for being angry with each other. Ask God to show you how you have hurt Juliet over the years to the point where she is no longer willing to talk to you. Then you must be willing to change yourself. Even if Juliet were totally in the wrong and you were completely in the right—which is seldom true in any marriage—all you can change is yourself."

Michael felt like he had missed something. "But how is that going to make Juliet willing to talk with me and work on the marriage?"

"When God shows you how you've hurt Juliet, you'll need to ask her to forgive you for those things you've done to let her down over the years. If she sees that you're willing to take responsibility for your share of the problem, I think she'll be more willing to work on the marriage."

Michael stood up to leave, and Ron came around the desk to hug him. "I want you to know, Michael, that I will be praying for you and Juliet in the weeks to come. Be sure to schedule a counseling appointment with my secretary tomorrow." He smiled warmly at Michael. "And don't give up. Remember that God is in the miracle business."

Chapter Fourteen

As one day merged into another, and Juliet found her time completely taken over by the care of her daughters, she was surprised to realize that almost two weeks had passed since Michael's departure. She knew that she should be concerned that they were living apart. But the truth was, she felt relieved to not have him there, adding his own sort of pressure to the stress she already felt from caring for two very sick girls.

Juliet had taken the girls to their family doctor on Tuesday, when they both still had fevers and occasional bouts of vomiting. Dr. Taylor confirmed Juliet's diagnosis of the flu, gave Heather some medicine for her nasty cough, and said that time would be the ultimate healer. In a perverse sort of way, Juliet was happy to be so consumed with the care of her children. She wasn't glad to see them feeling miserable, but it was a relief to be completely occupied with activities that had nothing to do with Michael or their marriage.

As usual, Sally had been a lifesaver, picking up groceries for Juliet so she wouldn't have to leave the girls. Sally had been curious when Juliet told her that Michael was staying with his old college roommate for a while, but they hadn't had the freedom to discuss it. When Sally stopped by with groceries, either her own kids were waiting outside in the car for her, or Daisy and Heather were listening.

The weather had been stormy and dreary all that Saturday afternoon, and Juliet had just lit a fire in the living-room fireplace for the girls. They'd been watching cartoons but had fallen asleep on their sofa beds. Daisy seemed to be getting better, but Heather had developed a cough deep in her chest and was still weak. Juliet was surprised when the doorbell rang and was delighted to find Sally standing on the front porch in the rain, holding a casserole dish.

"Aren't you a sweetheart! Do you have time to come in and drink something hot with me?"

"I was hoping you'd ask. Yes, John's home with the kids." Sally put her dripping rain slicker in Juliet's laundry room, and they sat down at the kitchen table with some mugs of hot herbal tea.

"Juliet, please don't take this as an insult, but when I stopped by with your groceries yesterday, I was shocked by how terrible you look. Are you eating or sleeping at all? You look like you're losing weight."

"Well, the girls only want to eat canned chicken soup, if anything. And I've been too busy and distracted to make myself a real meal. Thanks for bringing me some of your wonderful lasagna. That should help me get back a pound or two."

"Tell me honestly if you want me to mind my own business, but I'm concerned that Michael isn't here. Are you guys okay?"

"Remember when I went to the Dancercise convention two weeks ago? I met a nice man there—honestly, nothing really happened—and he took me to dinner. But it was so wonderful to sit at a restaurant and have a deep, meaningful conversation with an attentive man. After that night, something in me snapped, and I realized how dead my relationship with Michael had become. When I got home, I asked him to move out."

"What are your plans? Are you interested in this other man?"

"Oh no, not at all. He was nice, but I don't ever plan to see him again."

"Well then, are you going to get some counseling with Michael?"

"Michael has sent me a couple of cards this week. He said he's talked with Pastor Forsythe and is hopeful that we can turn things around. I'm just not ready to work on it with him."

"Juliet, isn't this what you've been hoping for? It sounds like you have Michael's attention. Why don't you want to work on your marriage?" Sally's voice sounded upset, but Juliet was too tired to care.

"I don't understand how I'm feeling, myself," she said

with a sigh. "You're right. For years I've done so many things to try to get Michael to take an interest in me. Now he wants to work on the marriage, and I don't think I have the heart for it. I guess he's broken my heart so many times, it may be dead now."

"I don't believe that. You're just worn out with the kids being sick. Get a few good nights of sleep, and you'll be yourself again."

"Sally, I'm afraid to trust him. I made him leave so that he would be motivated enough to deal with our messed-up marriage. Now he seems to care about fixing things, but I'm afraid that if I let him come home, he'll go back to shutting me out of his life again."

"You have to give it a chance. Maybe you've scared him enough to shape up for good."

After Sally left, Juliet heated up a serving of lasagna for herself. The girls were still asleep in the living room, and the house was quiet as she sat at the kitchen table and ate. She asked herself what was keeping her from feeling hopeful about the future of her marriage. When Michael had made love to her at Chaminade, she had enjoyed being close to him again physically, but now she realized that she wanted and needed much more than that. In her heart, she was still frustrated and unfulfilled. She felt like she didn't even know Michael anymore, and she didn't know if it would ever be possible to be truly intimate with a man who was so emotionally withdrawn.

A few minutes after she was done eating, she felt violently sick and ran to the downstairs powder room just in time to throw up. She looked at herself in the mirror above the sink as she rinsed out her mouth and splashed cold water on her face. Sally was right; she did look horrible. Her cheeks were sunken, and she was very pale, with dark circles under her eyes. She dreaded the thought that she had caught her children's flu bug. Who was going to take care of all of them, if she was sick, too?

As the evening progressed, Juliet felt increasingly miserable. Her head pounded, every bone in her body ached, and it hurt to swallow. The girls woke up and were surprised to find their mom huddled in a big quilt on the end of Daisy's sofa bed near the fire. Daisy seemed much stronger after her long nap, almost like her old self again. Juliet warned her that she thought she was getting the flu now, and Daisy assured her mom that she could take a turn playing nurse.

Juliet started out sleeping with Heather in her bed that night, but ended up lying on the bathroom floor with her pillow and a blanket so she could be closer to the toilet when she had to throw up. Finally, as daylight began to shine through the bathroom window, Juliet felt that she was done vomiting. She took a pan with her to her bedroom and crawled under her down quilt, shivering uncontrollably.

She knew that she must have a fever, but she was too weak and tired to get out of bed for some medicine, and she hesitated to take even a sip of water for fear that she'd be throwing up again. She fell asleep, only to be tormented by a frightening dream of losing Heathcliff and her girls on a hike in the woods. She woke up crying and calling for Heather and Daisy.

Daisy came in and stood next to her mother's bed with a worried look on her face. "Mommy, why are you crying?"

"I just had a nightmare. What time is it?" She felt so disoriented and was too exhausted to lift her head and look at the clock on Michael's side of the bed.

"It's about eleven o'clock. Don't worry about Heather and me. I made us some toast and cereal. We're downstairs watching TV. Are you okay?"

"I think I have the same thing you kids had. I just need to sleep. Will you come and talk to me if you need anything?"

"Sure, Mommy. Just go to sleep. We'll be fine."

Juliet really didn't have any choice. She could not remember ever being so sick before. She had caught the flu once in junior high, but she didn't think she'd felt this awful. The room seemed to be spinning, and the only way she could make it stop was to close her eyes and go back to the blissful blackness of sleep.

Sometime later, she felt a cool hand on her forehead and realized that Michael was standing next to the bed. She opened her eyes and saw a troubled look on his face. He looked as though he were about to cry. "How long have you been like this, sweetheart?"

"Since last night."

"What can I get for you? Maybe a cold drink or something to eat?"

"No. Please don't mention food. I threw up all night."

"Well, you'd better at least drink something or you'll get dehydrated," he warned.

Juliet started to cry. "I'm afraid to drink anything. I'm too weak to get up and dump out the pan if I get sick again. And I don't want to have Daisy do that for me."

"Juliet, don't worry about anything. I'm not going to leave you. I'll take care of everything." Michael went downstairs and returned with a cold washcloth for Juliet's head, some Tylenol for her fever, and a glass of ice water. Daisy followed him, carrying a dozen pink roses beautifully arranged in a vase. She set them down on the nightstand next to her mom's bed. Michael smiled at his wife. "Happy Valentine's Day, sweetheart. I'm sorry you're too sick to enjoy it."

Juliet was surprised that it was already Valentine's Day. She had been home with the girls for more than a week, except for the one trip out to Dr. Taylor's office. She must have become completely out of touch with the outside world to miss a holiday like Valentine's Day.

Daisy said, "He brought you a pretty box of candy, too, but since you're too sick, can Heather and I eat it?"

"Yes, I don't want it." Juliet was relieved to think that her daughters were well enough to be interested in candy again, but she didn't want the box in the room with her. Michael told Juliet to go back to sleep, and he and Daisy went downstairs.

Throughout that afternoon, Juliet slept fitfully. Once she woke up and saw Michael sitting on the love seat in front of their bedroom fireplace. He was staring into the flames, deep in thought, but looked over to the bed when Juliet called his name.

He asked her, "How are you feeling?"

"Terrible."

"You were crying and saying something in your sleep so I came up here to sit with you. Were you having nightmares?"

"I don't know. I didn't realize I was doing that. How are the girls?"

"They seem to be getting back to normal. If tomorrow weren't a holiday, I would say that Daisy is probably ready to go back to school. Heather is still coughing, but she says she feels much better. They both ate their dinner."

"Don't tell me what they ate. I can't think about food." She drank some water and fell back to sleep. The next time she woke up, it was the middle of the night and Michael was lying next to her in his old gray sweats, sound asleep on top of the covers. She realized that she was breaking a promise to herself by letting him stay when their issues had not been worked out, but she felt powerless to do anything else. Who would take care of their little girls? For the time being, Michael would have to stay. It would just make everything that much harder when she asked him to leave again.

Chapter Fifteen

The next morning, Michael was in the kitchen making French toast for the girls and thinking about how he would reschedule his week to take care of his family, when the phone rang. It was Bill, hoping for the best since Michael hadn't returned to the condominium the night before.

"Did Juliet decide to forgive you and let you come home for Valentine's Day?"

"Oh no. It was nothing like that. She's got the same flu that our kids have been sick with for a week. She can't even get out of bed."

"That's too bad."

"I'm sorry to see her so sick, but this may be an answer to prayer. After I've been here for a few days taking care of her, I can't imagine she'll want me to go again. Pray for us, Bill. I want to stay and work this out."

"You've got it, Mike."

Later in the day, everything changed when Juliet's dad showed up at their house unexpectedly. Leah had copied Leonard's phone number in England from a list on the front of the Nelson's refrigerator. When she'd returned to New York after her Christmas visit, she had called Leonard and told him to be praying for Michael and Juliet's marriage.

Juliet would never admit that anything was wrong when he talked to her on the phone, so Leonard had fallen into the habit of calling Jessica for updates. The last time he had spoken to Jessica, she had told him that Michael was staying with Bill, so he was surprised and encouraged when his son-in-law opened the front door.

"Dad! Aren't you supposed to be in England? What a surprise! Come in." Michael led his father-in-law into the kitchen. "I was just about to have some coffee. Do you want a cup?"

"No thanks, Michael. I drank too much of it on the flight over here. I just got in a few hours ago. Where are Juliet and the girls?"

"The girls are playing in their room, and Juliet is in bed with the flu."

"May I go up and say hi to everyone?"

Michael stayed in the kitchen while Juliet's dad went upstairs to surprise the family. He was thankful to have a father-in-law like Leonard. They had always had a positive, mutually supportive relationship with each other. But truthfully, he was frustrated that Leonard had come back from England early. Now it was unlikely that Juliet would want Michael to stay. Those suspicions proved to be right, as Michael discovered when he went up to check on Juliet a little while later. Leonard was down the hall, talking with his granddaughters in their room.

"Michael?" Juliet began tentatively. "Now that Dad is here, you'll be able to go back to Bill's and be safe from all our germs."

Michael was not going to be kicked out again that easily. "Why should we expose your dad to the flu? Doesn't he have to fly back to England soon?"

"He's planning to be in town all this week."

"If you and the girls give him the flu, he'll miss a lot more than a week of his sabbatical. I've already been exposed. Why risk your dad, too?"

"Michael, I'm too tired to debate this with you. The fact is, my dad is here to help me, and I don't want you to come home yet." Juliet was close to tears.

"What about what I want, Juliet? Since when did God put you in charge of this family?"

Juliet began crying, and Michael quickly decided that he didn't want to win the argument by taking advantage of his sick wife. "All right. I'm leaving. I'll call you later in the week." Michael went to his daughters' room to hug them and to say good-bye to his father-in-law.

He was furious as he left Mount Hermon, both with his wife and with himself. He didn't know how he would be able to break through her stubborn resistance. And he was angry with himself for not standing up to Juliet's unreasonable demands. How were they going to repair a damaged marriage if they were living apart? He decided to bury himself in his work while he figured out what to do next.

After Michael left, Leonard went into Juliet's bedroom to check on her and found her crying. When he asked what was wrong, she didn't want to discuss it with him. He reasoned that she would be more interested in talking when she wasn't feeling so miserable with the flu, so he went down to the kitchen and fixed dinner for his grandchildren.

Leonard's chance for a heart-to-heart talk with Juliet came two mornings later after he had walked the girls to the bus for their first day back to school since their illness. He took some tea and toast up to his daughter, who was propped up in her bed with a stack of pillows, and sat on a chair next to her bed while she ate.

"Dad, have I thanked you properly yet for coming to my rescue? I wouldn't have thought to pray for you to come and help. I figured you were stuck in England with William Shakespeare until the end of the summer, no matter what."

"I didn't realize you had the flu when I made the arrangements to fly home. I had just talked to Jessica last week and was concerned about your marriage."

"So Jessie was the tattletale; I should have figured."

"Actually, Leah Nelson called me at the beginning of

January and told me she was terribly concerned about you and Michael."

"Mom called you. All the way to Stratford, England. I can't believe she'd do that."

"Well, then you must not realize how distressed she is about your marriage. She knows I'm a praying man and wanted me to be asking God to help you. Leah is truly a lovely woman. It's a shame she lives in New York."

"Could this be possible, Dad? After all these years, do I hear you expressing interest in a woman? I guess the two of you share a love for Shakespeare and the theater."

"And we are both devoted to our children. I've had some delightful conversations with her in the last few weeks."

"Conversations? You mean she's called you more than once?"

"She called me the first time. And I've called her a few times since then. I'm going to have a two-day layover in New York when I leave here at the end of the week. Leah has gotten tickets for us to see a production of *The Taming of the Shrew.*"

"I'm stunned. This is the sweetest news I've heard in a long time."

"Now don't expect wedding bells or anything, but I truly enjoy Leah's friendship. She's looking forward to seeing me when I leave here. She's been half-sick with worry over you and Michael since she visited you."

"Well, I'm relieved that you showed up when you did; I wasn't ready to have Michael come home yet."

"Juliet, you have never explained to me why you don't

want Michael here with you. And I am upset that I had to find out you were in trouble through the grapevine like I did."

"Dad, all my life I've heard you talking about your dream of taking a sabbatical in England some day. I wasn't about to say anything to spoil this special time in your life."

"You should know by now that no matter what's happening in my life, you and Jessica are more important to me than anything. I've come a long way to help. Now will you tell me what's wrong with your marriage?"

Juliet looked at her dad's kind, concerned face and blinked back the tears that were ready to fall. He had always been so steady, so strong, and able to help her with any issue that life threw at her. But how could he relate to a bad marriage, when he'd never had one? Still, he was right; he deserved an explanation. "Dad, my marriage to Michael has been in trouble for a long time, and I thought that if I asked him to move out, maybe he'd have the motivation to work on it with me."

"How has it been in trouble?"

"Michael is always preoccupied with work, and he doesn't want to communicate with me. I feel like I've been married to a stranger for the past few years."

"Juliet, I think probably all married couples struggle with a lack of communication at least some times in their marriages."

"You and Mom didn't. You had a perfect marriage." She looked at him with such faith and sincerity that he hated to tell her the truth, but he knew it was time.

"Your mother and I didn't always have a wonderful marriage. We almost split up after Jessica was born."

Juliet pushed herself up higher on the stack of pillows behind her back, wondering if she had heard her father correctly. She shook her head as she said, "I can't believe that. You always seemed completely devoted to each other."

"By the time you were born, we had healed the rift between us, but when Jessica was a newborn, we went through a terrible time."

"What happened?"

"It was the classic new-baby crisis. Marie was completely absorbed with her new role as Jessica's mother and seemed to forget that she was also my wife. I was selfish and immature. I resented your mother for ignoring me and got involved with a young college professor."

"You mean you had an affair?" Juliet still couldn't believe what she was hearing.

Leonard let out a long sigh and looked down at the floor. "I'm ashamed to admit it, but yes, I did. When your mother found out, she threatened to leave me and probably would have if she hadn't been so concerned about trying to support herself and Jessica as a single mother. We decided to work out our problems for Jessica's sake. But for months we had little feeling for one another except anger and resentment."

"All the years I was growing up, I never saw a couple more in love than you and Mom. I'm having a hard time processing this."

"By the time you were born, Juliet, we did have a true understanding and devotion for one another. The only reason I'm telling you this now is to encourage you not to give up on Michael. I think it's common for every marriage to go through a difficult adjustment of one kind or another. How could two flawed human beings live happily together for their entire lives without problems?"

Juliet buried her face in her hands, feeling exhausted at the mention of Michael. "I'm just afraid to have him come home, Dad. I know Michael well enough to know that if he's living here with me and the girls, he'll have all sorts of emergencies at work that will get in the way of resolving our issues."

"Then don't invite him home yet. But don't give up, either. I know that you two love each other. Be patient and work on it." Leonard looked at Juliet's pale face with concern. He had never seen her so sick. "Darling, I can tell this conversation has worn you out. You're still very weak. It's not smart to take on the problems of life when you're down with an illness. Do us both a favor and park this problem while I'm here with you. When you've had a nice, long rest, God will show you what to do next."

Juliet had two more peaceful days of her father's spoiling and nurturing. She was able to spend most of her time in bed, resting and reading and regaining her strength. She still didn't have a normal appetite; many of the foods she had once enjoyed were suddenly repulsive to her. But she figured that was normal after the flu.

Saturday morning arrived, and Leonard kissed his daughter and his grandchildren good-bye. He planned on taking his car back to his townhouse in San Jose and getting a shuttle from there to the airport. It would be months before he returned. Juliet stood in front of the house with her girls and waved as he drove down the street and out of view. She walked back to the front door, silently thanking God for giving her such an incredible man for a father. He had been so unselfish to share his painful secret with her. Juliet felt that she owed it to her dad to try to work things out with Michael. She just wasn't sure how. How could she fix something when she didn't understand how it had gotten broken to begin with?

Chapter Sixteen

On Saturday evening, Juliet and the girls were playing Fish at the kitchen table when Michael walked in the door. He was dressed in a suit and had obviously just come from work. He smiled cautiously, as if to test the emotional waters with his wife. Daisy and Heather jumped up from their chairs and ran to the doorway to hug their daddy. He cuddled with them for a minute or two until Juliet intervened and told the girls that it was time for their bath.

"Mommy, I want to visit with Daddy," Heather whined as she clutched Michael around the neck.

Michael kissed her cheek and said, "Honey, I'll come up and read a bedtime story to you and Daisy after your bath, okay?"

At that suggestion, both girls hurried upstairs without a complaint. Michael sat at the kitchen table across from Juliet and looked at her with troubled eyes. "Can we talk please? Are you feeling better? You look so pale."

"I think I'm over the flu, but I'm still tired most of the time."

"Take it slow. I've never seen you this sick before." He cleared his throat and looked nervously around the kitchen, while Juliet braced herself for the dreaded request to move back home. "Juliet, I want to ask you a question. I went to look at a house today that a couple wants to put on the market. Their dog has just had a litter of puppies. They are brown-and-white miniature collies, and I thought of you. I know you'd love them if you went to look. Will you let me take you over there tomorrow afternoon? We could choose one, and they'll hold it for us until the puppies are old enough to leave their mother."

"Why do you want to do that, Michael? I didn't think you liked dogs. They need too much attention. Cats are more your style." She felt tears of rage building up in the back of her throat.

"Juliet, I know I can never make it up to you that Heathcliff is gone. But I think you're a happier person when you have a dog in your life. Maybe if you can get over the loss of Heathcliff, we can begin to fix our marriage."

"How can you think that I could even begin to replace Heathcliff with a new puppy? You still don't get it, do you? Our problems are not about Heathcliff; they're about us. About the way you don't want to share your heart and your life with me. About the way we never made love until I was practically begging you. Be honest with yourself, Michael. You weren't really interested in me until I asked you to move out, and you haven't been interested in years." She left the kitchen, afraid of what she might say if she didn't end the conversation. She took some deep breaths as she went upstairs to help the girls wash their hair.

Daisy and Heather were keyed up and arguing about which book they should ask their daddy to read to them. Finally, Juliet had heard enough of their bickering and told them she was sure their dad would be perfectly happy to read two books. She had just finished combing the tangles out of Heather's hair when Michael walked into the girls' bedroom. The freshly washed and shampooed little girls, in their matching pink nighties, began to jump on Daisy's bed chanting, "Daddy! Daddy!"

Michael looked pleased to be so popular with his daughters and grabbed Daisy to tickle her. The three of them piled on Daisy's bed, laughing and tickling each other, as Juliet walked down the hall to her room and shut the door.

Michael sat with his family at church the next morning, but Juliet would not agree to go out to lunch with him and the girls afterward. She said if he would take the girls to lunch, she would have a chance to get the house back in shape after being sick for more than a week. She was going back to her Dancercise classes the next day and didn't want to start a new week with the house in such a mess.

Daisy and Heather insisted that they had to eat at McDonald's, because they would be passing out wolf cub Teenie Beanie Babies that day with the Happy Meals, and the girls hadn't collected that one yet.

"Can't we choose a restaurant once in a while because the food is good, and not because we like the prizes that they're giving with the meals?" Michael asked his daughters as they tried to find an unoccupied table in the crowded restaurant.

"Daddy, this is our favorite food," Daisy insisted. "When we come here, we always eat everything you buy."

Michael realized that his daughter was right. He found a table in the far corner of the room near a window and sat down at the booth, across from his two pretty little girls. He smiled. "I've missed you both so much. I want you to know that, more than anything, I want to work out my problems with Mommy and come home again."

Daisy nodded her head understandingly, but Heather looked troubled. Tears filled her eyes, and her chin trembled slightly as she quietly asked, "Daddy, what if Mommy won't stop being mad at you? What if she never wants you to come home? Then what will you do?"

Michael's heart broke as he saw the worried expression on Heather's sweet little face. He wanted to wave a magic wand and tell her it was all a bad dream and that they could wake up and go back to their real, happy lives again. Instead he spoke strongly and confidently to his sensitive, younger daughter. "Heather, I have never loved anyone in my entire life the way I love your mommy. I'm staying away right now because I think that if we have this time apart, it will help us to get over our disagreement. But I don't plan to stay away from you or your mommy for very long. You three girls are the whole world to me."

His words seemed to reassure both girls. They finished their Happy Meals and went out to the Playland while Michael sat at the table, drinking his coffee and stewing. This separation could not go on much longer or his kids would be emotional wrecks.

Later, when he brought his daughters home, he found Juliet folding laundry at the kitchen table. She had gotten the house back to a neat and clean condition. She seemed to be relieved to have put away all the evidence of their two weeks of sickness and to have the cheerful rooms back to normal. The girls were upstairs, changing out of their church dresses, so Michael had a private moment with her.

"I'm concerned about the girls, Juliet. Heather was asking me at lunch why I wasn't back home yet, and she seemed upset."

"Oh, this is a new angle. Tap into my desire to be a good mother to my girls and make me feel guilty enough to ask you to come back." The sarcasm in her voice told Michael that she wasn't buying his story.

"So you think I'd be willing to use my own kids to manipulate you into changing your mind."

"You're the professional salesman, not me. The girls haven't indicated to me that they've been upset. When you did live here, you were gone most of the time anyway. And when you were home, you were usually on the phone. They might actually be getting more attention from you since you've moved out."

"You're not being fair. I don't want to talk about this now." He went upstairs to kiss his daughters good-bye and left through the front door without seeing Juliet again.

As Michael drove down to Santa Cruz, he wondered how he could possibly break through the high brick wall that Juliet had constructed between them. For the first time, he began to feel hopeless. Maybe too much damage had been done. But how would he ever explain to his precious little girls what had happened if he couldn't make peace with their mommy?

Michael's eyes filled with tears. He pulled over to the edge of the beach and parked his car in an empty parking lot. Oblivious of his expensive leather shoes and dress pants, he walked across the nearly deserted beach and sat down a few yards away from the pounding surf. The chilly damp air and the hard, cold sand that he sat on made little impression on him as he stared unseeing at the horizon.

He spoke in a whisper that only he and God could hear. "I'm out of ideas, Lord, and desperate for help. I can't understand Juliet. But unless I can see things the way she sees them, there isn't much hope for us to work this out. Please help me. Show me what I can't see." He sat there for over an hour, lost in thought, unaware of the passage of time. His every cell was pleading for God to intervene and to give him the wisdom and understanding that he needed.

As he looked out at the distant line where the gray blue

of the sky met the darker blue of the sea, scenes from his marriage began to replay themselves in his mind. But something different was happening as Michael recalled the events. Instead of remembering them from his perspective, he was seeing them through the eyes of his wife.

He remembered a night when he had come home upset because a couple he had been showing houses to for weeks had bought a place from one of his competitors. In spite of the late hour, Juliet had been waiting for him in their bedroom with a picnic set up on the floor in front of the fireplace. He had returned her hopeful smile with a distracted glance, never thanking her and hardly noticing the effort she had made to please him. Now on the beach, he felt her disappointment.

Then he recalled a day when he had made several phone calls to their mortgage banker, negotiating and finally pleading with him not to initiate a foreclosure on their Mount Hermon home. He had spent the rest of that day wondering where he would find the money to make a payment by the end of the week. When he came home that night, Juliet had met him in the garage, wearing a raincoat—and nothing else. His main reaction had been shock. The last thing on his mind at that moment had been sex. As Michael sat on the cold sand, remembering that night, he could feel Juliet's humiliation as he had laughed and treated her attempt at seduction as a joke.

Scene after scene replayed themselves in Michael's memory, destroying him with guilt and remorse. Finally, he remembered that hideous day when Juliet came in the door after a weekend in San Francisco with their girls. Michael could feel Juliet's panic and horror as she realized that Heathcliff had been left unattended in the front yard. He felt her grief and fury when she found her beloved dog dead on the side of the road. He experienced her loneliness and despair as she found a shovel in the garage to dig a grave for her loyal friend, alone, on a cold, dark night.

At that moment, Michael realized that his continued neglect of his wife had destroyed something precious and trusting in her, just as surely as his neglect had killed Heathcliff on the highway. Not only had he not been there for Juliet for years, but also he had allowed her devoted companion, who had always been there for her, to be killed.

Tears ran down Michael's face as he choked out his despair. "Oh, God! I don't blame her for hating me. I hate what I've done to her. Please don't let it be too late for me to make things right. Please forgive me for failing her as a friend and as a husband." He continued to sit, numb with grief, until the sun set behind the horizon.

Bill was engrossed in a Lakers game on TV and didn't look up when Michael came in the door. "Hi there! I saw you with your family at church. How are things going?" Bill turned to look at his friend when Michael didn't answer and was shocked to see that Michael had been crying. "What happened? Are you crying?"

"I've had a rough afternoon. I don't know how Juliet is ever going to be able to trust me again. I've been such an insensitive jerk."

"Stop it, Mike. It takes two people to wreck a marriage."

"Well, maybe I've made marriage history then, because in this situation, I have no one to blame but myself."

"Come on now, Mike. Sit here with me and watch the game. The Lakers are beating the Nuggets. Have you eaten anything?"

"I'm wiped out, Bill. I'm just going to bed." Michael trudged up the stairs on feet that were almost as heavy as his heart. He kicked off his shoes and stretched out on the lumpy single bed in Bill's guest room. Looking at his black kidskin shoes, which had been to him such a symbol of prestige and success, he now felt utter disgust with himself. Every spring and every fall, he would spend hours at Macy's and Nordstrom, sparing no expense to make himself look good for his prospective customers. When had he stopped caring about how he presented himself to his wife, the most important person in his life?

He had not found Juliet until he was thirty years old, and in all the years since their marriage, he had never found her equal. She had a way of making every little thing seem like a special occasion. Soup and sandwiches at dinnertime were presented like a feast because Juliet would take the time and effort to serve them on the prettiest plates and light candles on the table.

She took the same care with herself that she took with their home. She was just as lovely at thirty-three as she had been at twenty, when he had first met her. Her discipline wasn't limited to the way she dressed and the meticulous way she maintained her beautiful body; she was equally careful about the way she had continued to give herself to him as an interested and devoted lover—even long after he had given her no reason to be so attentive to him.

Michael suddenly remembered the time when he was in the fourth grade and had pleaded with his parents to buy him a pretty blue parakeet he had admired at the pet store. His parents had warned him that the bird would be his complete responsibility; they wouldn't be checking up on him every day to make sure that the cage was clean or that the bird had food and water. He had assured his parents that he would not neglect the little bird, who sang so sweetly. In the beginning, he had been enamored with the lovely pet. He had showed it off to all his friends and had taken great care to clean the cage and to check on the food and water supplies every day.

Then Little League season had come along, with all the after-school practices and weekend games. One morning when Michael woke up, he discovered that his beautiful blue bird was dead on the floor of the cage. When he looked more closely, he saw that the water dish was dry. So dry, that it had to have run out of water a long time before he discovered his loss.

As he remembered that poor trapped bird, who had been left to die with no resources to save itself, he realized that he had done the same thing to Juliet. From the earliest days of their relationship, Michael had been aware that Juliet thrived on romance and physical affection. As his wife, she couldn't go anywhere else to have those needs met. He admitted to himself that because of his pride and selfish desire not to seem inadequate to Juliet, he had cut off the supply of a thing that was as essential to her as food and water. He knew that Juliet would have been content to be kissed and cuddled during those long frightening months of his impotence. But he had denied himself all physical contact with her to protect his own ego. Now he wondered if it was too late to make things right with his irreplaceable Juliet, too late to recover his most valuable gift.

Chapter Seventeen

When Juliet's alarm clock went off on Monday morning, the last thing she felt like doing was getting out of bed, let alone teaching two Dancercise classes. She wondered how long it would be before she had her energy back. If she didn't start to feel like her old self again soon, it would be torture to teach six classes a week. She hung her head over a cup of strong black tea at the kitchen table and tried to console herself with the thought that she wouldn't have to teach again until Wednesday. Just then, Daisy came in for breakfast.

"Hi, Mommy. What's wrong?"

"I think this flu bug wants to make me miserable for a little longer. What do you want to eat?" Daisy asked for a Pop Tart, but as Juliet took it out of the toaster, a wave of nausea hit her, and she ran to the downstairs powder room in time to get sick. When she came back out, Daisy and

Heather were sitting at the kitchen table, looking at her with worried expressions.

"I'm not going to let this nasty bug get the best of me. I'm going to beat this thing!" She tried to sound strong as she smiled weakly at the little girls.

"Mommy, do you think you should go back to bed?" Heather offered. "I can bring a pan up for you."

"No, honey. I've got to get back to my Dancercise classes. I didn't ask anyone to cover for me today. We'd better hurry or you'll miss the bus." She asked the girls to get their own Pop Tarts, and they left on time.

By the time Juliet had finished her aerobics classes and returned home, she was dragging. She had not had anything to eat or drink all day except water and had taught two classes back-to-back. She decided to have a bowl of chicken noodle soup and a nap before the girls got home from school. As she opened the can of soup, the phone rang. It was her sister.

"Hi, Julie. Tomorrow night is the women's Bible study that you promised to try at least once with me. Remember?"

Juliet groaned. "Oh, Jessie, can't I play hooky for one more week? I'm still so beat."

"Listen," her sister reasoned, "you have to fix dinner for your kids tomorrow night, right? You and the girls can come here before the Bible study and I'll feed all of you, then Dan will watch all the kids while we go."

"Well, it would be nice to have someone else do the cooking. Food is still pretty repulsive to me. I'm afraid my poor girls will be losing weight because I can't bear to fix them a decent meal."

"Does that mean we're on?" Jessica asked hopefully.

"We're on. When should we be there?"

Heather and Daisy were delighted to be going to their aunt Jessica's house and seeing their cousins. The next afternoon, they were ready long before their mom. Juliet was having a hard time deciding what to wear. All of her favorite slacks looked too baggy since her weight loss. She decided on a long, burgundy, flower-print skirt with an elastic waist. Then she covered the loose-fitting waistband with an oversized burgundy sweater.

At the Parkers' house, while Juliet poured drinks for everyone and Jessica made some gravy to go with the pot roast, the two sisters had a chance to talk. "Were you surprised when Dad showed up on your doorstep last week?" Jessica wanted to know.

"Yes. His timing was so perfect. I didn't want Michael to stay, but there was no way I could have made it through last week without help. I was flat on my back."

"You still look a little sick. Have you been getting enough sleep? You look so pale." Jessica's eyes were troubled as she studied her sister closely.

"The girls got over it in a week and now act as if they've never been sick. I guess when you get older, it's harder to bounce back from the flu."

"Was Dad able to give you any marriage advice? He was so upset when I told him on the phone that you had asked Michael to move out. I hope you don't mind that I told him."

"No, I don't mind. It was such a blessing to have him with us last week. He is the sweetest grandpa, and he helped me in all sorts of ways. He cooked, entertained the kids, did the laundry, and yes, he did give me some marriage advice."

"What did he say?"

"He thinks I have to give Michael another chance. It's too soon to call it quits. Every marriage that lasts a lifetime goes through bad times. That sort of thing." Juliet had decided not to share her father's secret with her sister. As close as she was to her, she thought it was their father's place to tell Jessica the story of his affair long ago, if the time ever seemed appropriate.

"Are you going to take his advice?"

"Sure. I just thought I'd give it a little more time. Maybe I'll feel human again in a few more days." It took every ounce of energy she had just to handle the basic tasks of living with two little girls. She dreaded the thought of adding heavy, emotional discussions with Michael to her life.

"Oh, Jess, this was the best part of the visit with dad. Guess where he was headed when he left here? He's become close to Michael's mom, and he was stopping in New York for a couple of days to see her on his way back to England."

Jessica let out a shriek that brought Dan running to the kitchen to see if she had burned herself.

Later that evening as Jessica drove Juliet to the church that her family attended, she talked to her about the Bible study. "Ever since I went to Ruth's first class, I knew this was something that would help you with your marriage. I think this study would be good for any Christian struggling with life."

"Who is Ruth?"

"Ruth Moore is a beautiful Christian woman, probably in her fifties, with five grown children. She has always stood out in our church as someone with wisdom and maturity. A few of us who have admired her over the years asked her to lead a study group for us."

Jessica parked the car, and they made their way to the fellowship hall in the basement of the church. The twenty or so ladies in the class got their cups of coffee or tea, and Ruth asked them to open their Bibles to the book of Genesis. "Look in the third chapter, after Adam and Eve have sinned. In verse sixteen, God tells Eve that now her desire will be for her husband and he will rule over her. What does this mean to you? Years ago, I looked at that passage with a fresh understanding of how it applied to my life. I realized that in the original, perfect world that God created, a woman would look to God to meet all of her needs, not to her husband."

Ruth looked up from the pages of her Bible and smiled at the earnest faces of the women around her. "Let's put this in the context of our daily lives, ladies. How many of us in this room, if we are honest with ourselves, believe it is our husband's job to make us happy? How many of us come to our marriages with empty hearts and expect our husbands to fill them? I must tell you that it is vital for the health of every marriage for a woman to go to God to fill her heart. Then she can go to her husband as a giver, as a blessing. If you don't go to God with all your needs, you run the risk of depleting your husband emotionally and draining all the joy out of your relationship with him."

Juliet sat riveted to her seat during the hour and a half lesson and hurried to the front of the room to talk with Ruth afterward. The rest of the women were wandering over to a table set with tea and coffee and cookies.

"Ruth? Do you have a minute? I'm Juliet, and this is the first class I've come to. You said something tonight that has turned on a light in my head. What do you think happens in a marriage when a wife looks to her husband to meet all of her needs, instead of looking to God?"

"All I can tell you, Juliet, is what happened in my own marriage when I was younger. I expected my husband to be the romantic hero of my dreams and to help me through every emotional crisis that I faced. The dear man was being smothered to death, and it almost wrecked our marriage."

"How did you change?"

"I asked God to show me what I was doing wrong, and then I read that passage in Genesis and it hit me. I don't have to completely cave in to the curse we received after Adam and Eve's sin. I realize it will be a lifelong struggle, and my natural tendency will always be to want my husband to be and to do everything for me. But now I know that if I want to be happy, and if I want to have a good marriage, I'll go to God with my needs and concerns first, not to my husband. It's made a dramatic change in my marriage."

Tears came to Juliet's eyes, and she found herself pouring her heart out to this kind woman. "That's exactly what's been happening in my marriage. Poor Michael. I think I've put so many unrealistic demands on him."

"It's amazing, Juliet. When we stop needing so much from our husbands because we're allowing God to meet the desires of our heart, often we find that our husbands are suddenly there for us in ways they never were before."

"Could I please ask your advice on something? I haven't been able to bring myself to talk to anyone about this, and I would really like your opinion."

Ruth glanced around the room and saw that the other women were talking at the snack table, out of hearing range. "I'll be happy to help you, if I can."

"Recently, my husband told me that he has been under a lot of pressure at work, and I just learned that we've been in financial trouble for a long time. I was furious, because I thought he should have shared something major like that with me as soon as it happened."

"Juliet, I think that many men would be reluctant to share information like that with their wives. It doesn't mean that your husband doesn't love you. I would guess that his desire was to protect you."

"That's exactly what Michael told me. But how can I be close to him if he's keeping big secrets like that from me?"

"I can understand your desire to know about all the things that your husband finds stressful in his life. Just remember that men are not like us. Most of the women I know want to talk about the stress in their lives and get reassurance. Men have a powerful need to appear to be strong and capable. Have you ever been lost in the car with your husband?"

Juliet smiled at the memories Ruth's question conjured up. "Yes, many times."

"Most of us women will stop at the first gas station and ask for directions, while most men will wander around until they find their own way. It looks like pride to us. But I honestly believe they have a God-given instinct to be protective of their families. They need to look like they have everything under control, even when they don't."

"Do you think it can be too late to turn a marriage around when it's been in trouble for years?"

Ruth smiled and shook her head at her new student. "Dear, you promised God when you married your husband that you would stay together for better or for worse. You may be living through the 'for worse' part, but it can't be too late. If you're going to do God's will, then you have to stay together and work out your problems. Are you planning to continue coming to our Bible study?"

"Absolutely. I'm sorry I missed the first ones."

"Well, our main focus in the weeks ahead will be to learn ways to draw closer to God. I believe this is the solution to so many problems in our lives." Ruth put her hand on Juliet's arm and gave her a warm smile. "I want to encourage you, Juliet. I think you're going to find the strength and determination you need to work through any tough issues you're facing."

Juliet sat quietly in her sister's car, deep in thought, as they headed toward Jessica's house. Finally, Jessica broke the silence, asking Juliet if she had gotten anything useful out of the class.

"Jessie, thank you for making me come with you tonight. I think I've just gotten an answer to a prayer I've been praying for a long time. But I don't know how I'm going to change. I've been making bad choices for such a long time."

"Does this mean that you're going to ask Michael to come home?"

"I think what I need to do for the time being is spend time alone with God. I need to learn how to depend on God for everything before I go running to Michael. It will be a whole new way of managing myself as a wife, but I honestly believe it's what I have to do. I want to learn how to be happy and complete within myself and to stop being so needy."

"Ruth is a wonderful teacher. I've learned so much since I've been going to her classes."

"What amazes me is that all this time I've been telling myself that Michael has been letting me down as a husband. I have been feeling so sorry for myself and blaming him for ignoring me, when I know his job is incredibly stressful. Instead of being thankful for how hard he works to provide for us, I constantly complain about his work, like a spoiled child. It never occurred to me until tonight that I could be a big part of our problem."

"So will you be coming with me to the study every week?"

"I wouldn't dream of missing it. I'm sorry I've missed so many classes already. Maybe you can fill me in with your notes."

Chapter Eighteen

When Heather came home from school on Wednesday, she had a note from her first-grade teacher, Melanie Barrett. Juliet wondered what the note could be about. She hadn't realized that Melanie had returned from her emergency family leave. Mrs. Barrett was a Mount Hermon neighbor of theirs and two years ago had taught Daisy in first grade. She lived a little farther up Pine Avenue than Sally and John. From some conversations they'd had, Juliet knew that Melanie was a Christian.

Melanie's husband had been killed in a snowboarding accident at Lake Tahoe around the middle of January, and she'd been on leave from school ever since. Juliet knew that Heather must be delighted to have her beloved teacher back and was surprised her little girl hadn't mentioned it. Ever since the first week of school, Heather had been devoted to the gentle and patient Mrs. Barrett.

Juliet had worked as a volunteer in Melanie's class once a week when Daisy had been a student of hers. This year, Juliet was helping Mrs. Barrett and her students again but had missed the past three weeks because of the family's flu battles. She normally volunteered in Melanie's class on Tuesday mornings and re-shelved books in the school's library on Thursday afternoons.

Yesterday, she had sent a note to school with Heather, explaining that she wasn't well enough to help that day. She had woken up on Tuesday morning to another spell of vomiting and was afraid she still might be contagious around a class full of first graders. She had spent most of Tuesday in bed before she had gone to the Bible study with Jessica.

Now Juliet took Melanie's note from Heather, who acted nervous, as if she was afraid that she might be in trouble.

Hi Juliet,

I'm sorry you've been sick with the flu. If you're well enough to come to school tomorrow to work at the library, will you stop by my room at the end of the day? I'd like to talk with you about something.

Take care,

Melanie

"Heather, Mrs. Barrett just wants me to come and talk to her when I'm done working in the library tomorrow. How long has she been back at school?"

"She came back on Monday."

"You must be so happy to have her teaching you again." Juliet knew that Heather had not liked the grouchy substitute teacher the school had found to fill in for Melanie after her husband's death.

"Yeah. Can I go and play now?"

"May I go and play. Yes, honey."

It would be easier to talk with Melanie candidly if her girls weren't tagging along. She usually drove them home from school on Thursdays after she volunteered, so Juliet called Sally to ask if her girls could go there after school the next day.

The next afternoon, Juliet arrived at Melanie's classroom just as she was lining up the children to meet their buses. Juliet walked over to Heather and hugged her. "Remember, honey, go to Mrs. Day's house with Daisy and Katie. I'll pick you up there on my way home."

Juliet watched with silent admiration as the delicate blond teacher patiently helped a disorganized little boy find his coat and put some take-home papers into his backpack, which was smeared with peanut butter. Then Melanie gave a hug and some words of encouragement to a tearful little girl who couldn't find the Beanie Baby she had brought in for show and tell. Finally, she shepherded all her little students out to their respective buses.

A few minutes later, she came back to the classroom,

not looking the least bit harassed, and sat down at her desk with a smile for Juliet. *Fragile* was the word Juliet would use to describe this slender, pale-blond beauty with the china-blue eyes. She looked older now with her recent sorrow. Yet there was a quiet strength and self-assurance in this sweet lady that caused Juliet to respect her, rather than pity her.

Melanie smiled at her guest. "I'm glad you're feeling well enough to be here today."

"Melanie, I want you to know how sorry I am about Alan's death. How are you doing? Is it hard to be teaching again?"

"I stayed home for more than a month, as you know, but being alone wasn't helping me after a while. I think keeping busy with the kids is going to be better for me. What you probably don't know is that I found out I'm pregnant shortly before Alan died. That's almost as hard for me to handle as his death." She took a deep breath and was quiet for a minute. "I waited and longed for a baby for years. Now that the baby is coming, my husband is gone."

Juliet was horrified by what she was hearing. She could only imagine how depressed this poor woman must be feeling. "When is your baby due?" she quietly asked.

"September. This will probably be my last year of teaching for many years to come. Maybe I'll come back when my baby is old enough to be in school all day with me." She smiled weakly.

"You won't have to work to survive financially?"

"No. Fortunately money isn't a problem."

"Have you been getting support from your family or church friends?"

"The only family I have now are my in-laws, who live in Delaware, and an aunt, who lives in Texas. My own parents died three years ago. But yes, my church family has overwhelmed me with their love and concern. By the way, thank you so much for the beautiful flower arrangement you sent for Alan's funeral. It was so cheerful—lovely spring flowers."

"It was such a minor thing to do. I had planned to bring over a casserole or something, after all your out-of-town guests had gone home. I heard you had a house full of company for a while. But then we all came down with the flu. I wish I had helped you more."

"Please don't feel the least bit guilty, Juliet. I have so much food and so many frozen casseroles in my freezer right now, I could have an open house for the entire neighborhood and not run out of food. But I didn't ask you here to talk about me. I wanted to ask you about Heather. Is she acting differently at home?"

"No. Why do you ask?"

"Since I've been back at school this week, I've found her in tears a couple of times at her desk. When I ask her what the trouble is, she doesn't want to talk. Then the other day at recess, I found her sitting by herself on a bench. Again, she looked like she was about to cry, and she didn't want to talk or play. That's not like Heather at all. I'm concerned that she's upset about something."

"My husband moved out of our house at the beginning of the month. We're having some problems in our marriage." Juliet spoke the words quietly.

"So you've been living with your own crisis these past few weeks." Melanie looked at Juliet with eyes full of sorrow and understanding.

"I'm hoping that we'll be resolving things in the next few days. Michael has gotten some counseling, and so have I. We just haven't decided that it's time to work things out under the same roof."

"And I guess Heather is really missing her daddy."

"I feel terrible that I haven't been sensitive to how unsettled she must be because of our problems. Daisy seems to be going along as if nothing is different."

"But Daisy is much more direct and assertive. She doesn't silently mull over things, the way Heather does. If Daisy were upset, I'm sure she'd tell you. Heather is probably afraid to burden you with her fears."

Juliet's eyes filled with tears. Finally she choked out, "I wonder what kind of long-term damage I've done to those poor kids. I have been so selfishly absorbed with my anger and my issues, I haven't thought enough about them."

Tears filled Melanie's eyes as well. "Juliet, you can help your daughters get over their fears and sadness when your husband comes back to live with you. My baby will never get to live with his father."

"Oh, Melanie. My heart is broken for you. But I don't want to be so negative about the fact that you're having a baby. There is no doubt that your child will be the greatest blessing in your life. I just wish you could share the fun and joy with Alan."

"I don't know what your issues with Michael are, Juliet. You don't need to tell me. But don't take his fatherhood for granted. My dad meant so much to me when I was growing up. And even if they're not complaining to you, I know your little girls will be relieved to have their father back home."

Juliet was afraid that if she answered Melanie, she would burst into tears, so instead she got out of her chair and went around the desk to hug her. What a gift this grieving widow had given her—the gift of a proper perspective on her problems.

Melanie told Juliet that she would walk out to the parking lot with her. As she pulled her purse from her desk drawer, she asked Juliet which pediatrician she took the girls to. "When I saw my obstetrician, she recommended that I find a doctor for the baby before he's even born."

"You said 'he.' Do you know, then, that your baby is a little boy?"

"No. I don't know for sure. But ever since I found out I am going to have a baby, I've always thought of it as 'he.'"

"Well, to answer your question, we all go to Dr. Taylor. He goes to our church. He isn't actually a pediatrician; he's a family practitioner. We all love him, though. He's funny and kind and very patient with all my questions."

"Thanks for the lead. I'll have to look him up. I guess I still have some time, though. September seems far away right now."

"Melanie, you know I live right down the street from you. Will you promise to call me if you need anything? I really want to help you through this." Juliet stooped down next to the open doorway of Melanie's car as Melanie pulled on her seat belt. "I'm so happy you're going to be a mother. You have such a gift with children."

As Juliet walked over to her car, something about her conversation with Melanie kept running through her mind. No doubt it was a long shot, but she decided to go to the drugstore before she went to pick up the girls.

Juliet stopped at her own house before she went to Sally's. She wanted to be alone when she took the pregnancy test. She wondered why the possibility of being pregnant hadn't occurred to her until she'd talked to Melanie, but as she looked at the calendar, she realized that her period was more than a week late. Michael had surprised her when he had rented a room for them at Chaminade, and she hadn't taken her birth control with her.

As she stood next to the bathroom sink and watched two little lines appear across the pregnancy test wand, she felt as if she were in a dream. She didn't know whether to laugh or to cry. But after her sad conversation with Melanie, she could only feel thankful that her husband was alive and would no doubt be there to support her through this pregnancy. Maybe this was God's way of telling Michael and her that their marriage still had possibilities.

She wondered how she was going to keep such a big secret to herself when she went to pick up Daisy and Heather at Sally's a few minutes later. But she was determined that no one would hear this news before she told Michael.

A short while later, Juliet knocked on the Days' door and walked into the kitchen. Sally grinned at her and said, "You look happy. Did your meeting go well?"

"Yes. Melanie Barrett is such an excellent teacher. I'm really thankful that both of my girls got her for the first grade."

"We were all pleased with her nurturing and kindness when Katie had her last year. Maybe Johnny will be in her class, too, in a couple of years."

"She just told me this will be her last year of teaching for a while. She's going to have a baby in September."

Sally gasped in dismay. "Oh, but her husband just died!"

"I know. Can you imagine how lonely she must feel right now? Sally, I've just had a major reality check. I have so much to be thankful for. I am going to go home, clean and cook up a storm, and then ask Michael to please come back to us. Whatever problems we have to deal with are nothing compared to Melanie's."

Sally smiled her approval. "You are definitely on the right track, Juliet. So do you think Michael will be back this weekend?"

"I want to fix everything at our house really nice and go to his office after my Dancercise classes tomorrow. I'm going to ask him to forgive me for being so stubborn. He's been wanting to come home for weeks."

Daisy and Heather were thrilled to help Juliet get the house straightened up for their daddy's return. They cleaned their room, sorted piles of dirty laundry, and dusted for their mom. Juliet heated frozen burritos in the microwave that night for dinner so she could spend time making a big pot of Michael's favorite beef stew. She wanted to have most of her weekend chores out of the way so that when Michael came home the next night, she would be free to focus on him and the girls.

Juliet was amazed at how feeling positive about life again had given her such a burst of energy. Now that she knew her nausea and tiredness were because of a precious new baby and not the lingering effects of the flu, she felt a surge of well-being that completely surprised her. She was going to have an infant to love and care for again. She wondered why she had ever had reservations about becoming pregnant a third time. She couldn't imagine anything she'd rather do at this point in her life than have another baby with Michael.

That night as she tucked the girls into bed, she asked them if it had been hard for them to have their daddy living in another house. Daisy was the first to volunteer her point of view. "I knew you would stop being mad at each other pretty soon. Daddy told us at McDonald's that he never loved anyone the way he loves you."

Juliet's heart skipped a beat at her daughter's words. "I feel the same way about Daddy. He is the most wonderful man I've ever known. Heather, have you been sad to have Daddy away?"

"Sometimes. I like it when he throws baseballs with us while you're fixing dinner. Will he do that again, Mommy?"

"Sweetheart, I know your daddy has been missing the ball throwing as much as you have. You're going to have to practice a lot because Little League season is just around the corner."

She prayed with her children and kissed them good night. As she walked down the hall to her own room, she smiled at the thought that she would be sharing a bed with her husband again the next night. She wasn't even wondering whether or not they would make love; she was trusting God to make that satisfying again, in his own perfect time. She just wanted to have Michael home.

Chapter Nineteen

After Juliet's classes the next day, she nervously prepared to visit Michael at his office. She showered and changed into a pretty blue-and-green-flowered shift and a matching blue cardigan. Then she painstakingly redid her makeup and brushed her hair so that it fell straight down her back. Slipping on her brown high-heeled sandals, she grabbed her oversized brown leather tote bag, locked the door of the dance studio, and went out to the sidewalk along the Pacific Garden Mall in Santa Cruz.

As she hurried toward the parking garage, she suddenly realized that Michael was sitting on a park bench in front of her building. "Hey! What are you doing here? I was just on my way to your office."

He smiled tentatively at her. "Boy, that's good to hear. I was hoping you'd be happy to see me and wouldn't hit me with your tote bag."

She looked into his handsome hazel eyes and smiled in return. "As a matter of fact, I'm delighted to see you, Michael."

"Well in that case, can I talk you into a cup of coffee at the bakery down the street?"

"Make it tea, and you're on." She still loathed the thought of coffee.

"That's easy enough. You're still not over the flu, huh?" He looked concerned as they walked to the quaint European bakery. Even though it was almost one o'clock in the afternoon, the little café was not very crowded. Michael asked the waitress to give them a quiet table in the corner, and then asked Juliet if she'd like a sandwich to go with her tea.

"No. I just want to talk right now. I'm not interested in food."

Michael ordered two pots of herbal tea for them, and after the waitress walked away, he turned to his wife with a troubled look. "Juliet, we've got to find a way to help you get interested in food again. You look like you've lost a lot of weight, and if you don't regain your strength, you'll just be getting sick again."

"Don't worry, Michael. I really am feeling better. I'm just so focused on what I want to say to you that I don't want to be distracted by food."

"I'm all ears."

"First of all, God has made it plain to me that I need to ask for your forgiveness."

"What! That's outrageous!" He blurted the words out

loudly and then quickly glanced around at the other tables. No one was paying attention to them.

"Michael, you've been asking me to work out our issues with you for weeks now. Do you want me to tell you what I think?" She spoke with quiet determination, and he nodded in agreement.

Juliet stared down at her hands. "I went to a Bible study with Jessie at her church, and I learned something that has completely transformed my thinking. We had a wonderful, wise woman for our teacher. She told us that one of the biggest traps wives fall into is that they expect their husbands to fulfill all their dreams and wishes. That's completely unrealistic. She said that we want things from our husbands that are only fair to expect from God, not from any normal human being. I know I've done that to you all the years we've been together, and I'm asking you to please forgive me."

When Juliet looked up to see Michael's response, she was shocked to find tears running down his face. "Michael, what is it? Why are you crying?"

He answered quietly as he wiped away his tears with a paper napkin. "I don't deserve an apology, Juliet. I'm the one who should be begging your forgiveness. You've done nothing wrong."

"That's not true, Michael. I've been a spoiled brat, feeling sorry for myself and angry with you most of the time. And all because you've been so busy working to keep us in our extremely comfortable lifestyle. I've expected you to come in the door from a stressful day at work and completely zero in on me and my fantasies. I have been so selfish and unfair. But I want you to know I've promised God that with his help, I plan to grow up and become a real wife and maybe even a friend to you."

"I'm amazed at what you're saying. Juliet, I have had such an agonizing week. God has had me by the scruff of the neck and has been showing me how I've failed as a husband over and over again. First of all, I've let you down by not leading our family spiritually. I don't even pray with you. It scares me to realize that the thought of praying with you was embarrassing. We are supposed to know each other better than any two people on earth, but I've been acting like I'm still a bachelor, always shutting you out."

He looked at her intently, and she had never believed in his sincerity more than she did at that moment. Now it was her turn to have tears running down her cheeks. She reached into her tote bag for a tissue and wiped away her tears. "It looks like God has been dealing with both of us this week. I'm overwhelmed by the changes he's made in our hearts in just a few days."

Michael nodded in response. "Juliet, it's been so hard not to call you all week. God brought me to my knees on Sunday after I left you and the girls. I just didn't think I should talk to you until I did some intense soul-searching. Finally, I understood what I needed to be and to do in order to fix our marriage. I just had to search my heart, to know whether or not I had the guts to make the changes I'm going to have to make."

"I think I know how you feel. After I went to the Bible

study on Tuesday night and found out what I was doing to wreck our marriage, I wanted to call you right away and apologize. Then I realized it would be premature to apologize if I didn't think I had it in me to be a different kind of wife—a less demanding and more understanding wife."

"Sweetheart, you've been an amazing wife. I've always known how blessed I am to have you. When I think of all the times I've taken you and your thoughtful romantic surprises for granted, I feel sick."

She looked into his eyes with all the love that was welling up in her heart. Then Michael looked at his watch, and she felt a familiar letdown. She figured he was thinking that it was time to get back to his office. Well, this is real life, she scolded herself. After all, it was a business day and they had a lot of bills to pay.

"Juliet, it's only quarter of two. When do the girls come home from school?"

"In about two hours."

"Okay. How about this? I'll race you home to our bedroom. The last one there has to lock the door and take the phone off the hook. Where's your car parked?"

"In the parking garage." She blushed and smiled nervously. She felt as if she were twenty-one years old again.

"Well, it's still kind of fair, because even though you have to walk farther to your car, I'll stay here and pay the bill. That way you'll get a head start." He grinned at her, and once again he was the Michael she had fallen in love with on the beaches of Kauai.

Chapter Twenty

Juliet deliberately took her time as she walked to her car. Then she used a slightly roundabout route to leave the downtown Santa Cruz mall area. She wanted Michael to beat her home. The feeling of being desired again by her husband was so incredibly delicious that she didn't want to do anything to take the initiative away from him. She delighted in the fact that, once again, he was making the first move, and she was responding.

As she drove on the freeway back to Mount Hermon, she thanked God repeatedly for the dramatic changes he had brought about in her life in just a few days. She was terrified that she would do something to ruin the sweet understanding that she and Michael seemed to have reached. Then she reminded herself that God didn't give her a spirit of fear. As long as she allowed God to be in charge of every aspect of her life, she felt confident that things would only continue to get better.

Juliet saw Michael's BMW in the driveway as she pulled into the garage. As agreed, she locked the front door and took the phone off the hook, then walked up the stairs to their bedroom. She felt almost as nervous as she had on their wedding night. She took a deep breath, willed her heart to stop racing, and prayed silently that things would go well.

Michael was waiting for her. For the first time in years, the sensual opulence of the decorations they had chosen for their bedroom so long ago didn't mock her; it seemed completely appropriate.

After Michael made love to Juliet, he insisted on serving her lunch in bed. He came back upstairs after a quick trip to the kitchen, carrying a tray loaded with food. He served cream cheese and crackers, a bowl of fresh fruit, and a pitcher of ice water. Juliet was relieved that all his choices appealed to her newly finicky taste buds. She didn't want to discourage Michael by not eating the lunch that he had prepared.

As he spread cream cheese on wheat crackers and covered a plate with them, he shared his fears with Juliet. "Sweetheart, I really want to be there for you and the girls, but I've been indulging in bad habits for so long, I'm not sure how to change. Do you think you could remind me when I'm starting to get withdrawn and shutting you out? I know now that's like cancer to a marriage."

"What, like have a secret code that only we know? Something like, I wonder how Bill is doing these days?" she teased.

"Yes! That would be perfect. One thought of going back to Bill's will turn me around in a heartbeat."

"Was it that horrible? I thought he had a nice, new condominium."

"It wasn't the condo or Bill. They're both great. I'm just spoiled by you and our family. I would be miserable in a five-star hotel if I wasn't with you."

"Oh, Michael, I'm glad you want to be accountable to me. I hope you won't regret it."

He reached over and hugged her. "Never," he promised.

When they finished their lunch, Michael suggested moving down to the kitchen so that they could eat some ice cream. She followed him down the stairs but decided on tea rather than risk the ice cream. They sat at the table together, dressed in old sweats, like a couple of kids playing hooky from school. The microwave buzzed, signaling that Juliet's mug of tea was ready. Michael insisted on getting it for her and then asked, "Remember that night at Chaminade, when you told me you never cared where we lived?"

"Sure, I remember that night. I've been asking myself what I did to make you feel like you couldn't tell me about our money problems. I realize that I can be dramatic, and I tend to overreact to things."

"Juliet, I meant what I said that night. I didn't tell you about the financial problems we're having because I was trying to protect you."

"I believe you, Michael. But I hope that someday you won't feel like you need to protect me from information like that. We have God, and I have you. I don't need any better protection than that."

"I've decided that if being the kind of husband and father I want to be means I have to work fewer hours or even change jobs, I'm determined to do it."

She couldn't believe her husband was talking like this. It thrilled her to think that he was willing to try to get some balance in his life. "Michael, there are so many extravagant ways we spend money. I bet if we looked at our budget, we'd find all sorts of ways to save. But if living in this house means you have to keep working so hard, I think we should move."

"Juliet, you've always loved this house, even before you met me."

"I'd have to have rocks in my head not to love this house and Mount Hermon. But I don't love it more than I love you, Michael. This place means nothing to me, if you're not here. I found that out these past few weeks."

"Let's pray that we can find a healthy balance in our life and stay here, too. I've actually been surprised at how well I've done with sales this past month. I didn't work as many hours as I usually do, and most of the time I was completely out of it mentally because I've been so upset." He shook his head at the awful memories. "I have never seen you that stubborn. I was afraid I'd never be able to reason with you again."

"By the way, I owe you another apology. On Sunday, I

thought you were trying to manipulate me by saying that Heather was upset because you had moved out. Well, her teacher called me in for a meeting at school yesterday and told me the very same thing. I'm sorry I doubted your instincts, Michael."

"I don't blame you for not trusting me, sweetheart. When I look back over the past few years, I have to face the fact that I haven't done much to earn your trust or your love. I have missed Daisy and Heather so much. I guess I didn't realize how much I love being their dad until I couldn't be here with them."

She smiled tenderly at him. "They were so excited last night when I told them I was going to go to your office and ask you to come home. They helped me clean the whole house before they went to bed."

"You've sure had your hands full this past month, trying to be a single parent while everyone had the flu. I intend to spoil you for a while and see if you can gain some weight back. If you're still not back to normal after that, I'm taking you to see Dr. Taylor. When I was hugging you a little while ago, I could feel your ribs. You've got me scared, Juliet."

"I think I will be gaining some weight soon. In fact, I'm sure of it. But I'll need to see a doctor, anyway. Michael, remember when I met you for dinner at Chaminade?"

"Of course I remember that night." He looked into her gorgeous blue eyes and smiled at the memory.

"I thought we were just going to eat dinner. I didn't know you had booked a suite for us."

"I wanted to surprise you."

"Did you realize I left my birth control home that night?" Now it was her turn to grin mischievously.

"You mean? . . . Really?"

"Yes, darling, another baby is on the way."

"Oh, Juliet!" He jumped off his chair and started to pace around the kitchen, grinning all the while like the Cheshire cat. Then he turned to her with a sudden question, "Are you happy about this? I mean you've got a lot more freedom again with the girls both in school. Now you'll be back to diapers and middle-of-the-night feedings."

"Honey, of course! How could I not want to have another baby with you? Our first two have been so precious. This is just one more confirmation to me that we are on the verge of the best part of our marriage. I feel so blessed."

"But what about teaching Dancercise classes?"

"It looks like we'll both be making some job adjustments in the next few months. Michael, there is nothing I love more than being your wife and raising our children. Maybe someday I'll go back to teaching aerobics and lead the first class of Dancercise for senior citizens." She giggled at the thought.

"Even when you're an old lady, there will never be another woman more attractive to me than you."

"I feel the same way about you. You can still make my heart turn over with just a look. Listen, before the girls get home, I need to eat a little more crow."

"Juliet, stop! You've apologized enough for one day. No matter what it is, I forgive you."

"I've been thinking about those puppies you were telling me about."

"I've never seen anything cuter. Do you want to go and see them?"

Juliet sighed and shook her head, "Sheba will probably never forgive me for bringing an energetic puppy into her sedate life, but I love the idea of having a dog to go with me on my walks through the neighborhood with our new baby. If we get one soon, he could be housebroken before baby number three arrives on the scene."

"I'd love to get you another dog. Wait till we tell the kids! A new baby and a new puppy." The doorbell ringing almost drowned out his words.

"That's the girls. Let's save the news about the baby until after we see the doctor. I think hearing about the puppy will be exciting enough for them for the time being. And once we tell them, the whole world will know." Juliet hurried to the front hallway to let their daughters in.

"Hi, girls. Come and see Daddy in the kitchen. We have some exciting news for you."

"Daddy! Daddy!" Heather called out and ran into the kitchen ahead of her mother and big sister.

While Michael and the girls ate after-school snacks and took turns suggesting names for puppies, Juliet went upstairs and stretched out on her bed. Suddenly, she felt completely exhausted, as if she had run a marathon. She fell asleep and woke up to find Michael sitting on the side of the bed.

"Sweetheart, I want to take you and the girls out for a celebration dinner tonight, okay? Did you have any special plans for dinner?"

"Well, I made some of your favorite beef stew last night, but it will keep for dinner tomorrow. What did you have in mind?"

"How about Chaminade? Daisy and Heather have never been there. And I feel indebted to the place when I think that we owe our newest family member to their hotel."

She smiled at him while she stretched and tried to wake up. "Honey, are you forgetting our money problems? I think McDonald's would be more in order."

"Maybe, but this is a special day. I want us to go somewhere really nice to celebrate."

"Let's celebrate and not spend too much. How about the Santa Cruz Harbor? That's where we went for our first date. I don't mean the Crow's Nest, but maybe we could get some seafood at one of those little restaurants on the wharf."

"Yeah. I think you're right. The girls will like that. They enjoy talking to the sea lions under the wharf."

Michael was so attentive as they went out for the evening, that Juliet kept asking herself if this was just one long, lovely dream. Was this man who was opening her car door and holding her hand as they walked along the wharf really Michael?

After Michael had ordered their dinner, he turned the discussion back to good names for a dog. The girls were thinking along the lines of physically descriptive names like Copper, Goldie, and Fluffy.

"Heathcliff was a proper, elegant name for a beautiful dog," Michael said, looking intently at Juliet. He didn't want to stir up heartbreaking memories, but he wanted to get a feel for why Juliet was so quiet and detached. "I think we should choose a name that's dignified, like Heathcliff's name was. What do you think, Juliet?"

"I always like to meet the pet before I pick a name. I'll have to see his face and get a feel for his personality. Daddy says these dogs look like Lassie, from the movies, so maybe we could call it Lassie, if it's a girl, or Laddie for a boy."

The girls were still in a heated debate about names when Juliet was getting them ready for bed a few hours later. She finally quieted them down after reading them two bedtime stories. When she got into bed, she was surprised to find Michael awake.

"Isn't this kind of late for you, honey?"

"I didn't want to go to sleep without kissing you good night. I've missed that these past weeks."

"I don't mean to discourage you, but you haven't been in the habit of kissing me good night for years now. Is this something new?"

"Juliet, I was such a fool, taking what we had for granted. I don't think I'll ever be the same again."

As Michael kissed her good night and fell asleep, holding her close to his chest, Juliet prayed silently that neither of them would go back to the way they had been.

An hour later, Michael was sound asleep and snoring

softly, but Juliet's mind and emotions were churning. She actually felt sick with fear and dread and knew she wouldn't be able to sleep. She eased out of bed, pulled on her ancient, blue, terry cloth robe, and quietly went downstairs. It was time for another midnight meeting with God out on the back deck.

She sat on the porch swing, remembering that the last time she'd prayed there in the dark, Heathcliff had been keeping her company. Tears poured down her face as she longed again for her loyal friend.

She looked up at a lonely star and spoke aloud into the black night air. "Oh, Father, I'm so afraid. I'm just so afraid. And I miss Heathcliff. Will that ever go away?" The pain and fear were so big in her heart, that she was at a loss for words and just sat there quietly for a long time, crying in the dark.

Suddenly she felt a strong hand on her shoulder and realized that Michael was there. "What is it, sweetheart? What's going on?" He sat next to her on the swing and put his arms around her as she laid her head on his chest and sobbed.

"Oh, Michael, I'm so afraid. I've waited and prayed for this moment for so long, and now I'm afraid it won't last. How are we going to keep from getting into trouble again?"

"Of course we're going to get in trouble and have problems again, Juliet. Every couple does. But we'll work it all out. I love you, and I know you love me. Our kids are depending on us, and now we're going to have another little one who's going to need us to do the right thing."

"But don't you see, Michael? We've never figured out why you didn't want to share your heart with me to begin with. And there's something else you may not know. After Heathcliff died, my feelings for you turned completely cold. I am terrified to admit that for a long time I honestly didn't care whether we stayed together or not. How could I just turn off completely toward you when I've loved you for so long? We don't know how we got so messed up before, so how can we keep from getting messed up again?"

"That's a good question, and to answer it, we're going to need some help. I've known that for a few weeks now. Just because we're back together doesn't mean our problems have gone away. I'm hoping that you'll come with me for counseling with Pastor Forsythe. He's been wanting to talk to us as a couple."

"Does he think that he can help us?"

"According to Ron, our problems are about as common as a cold. He told me awhile back, though, that we should meet with him together. You just weren't in the mood to do that until now." Michael looked at her and smiled, and she was comforted by the strength and confidence she saw in his eyes. "Don't worry about anything, Juliet. I honestly think we're going to look back at this time in our marriage someday and see it as a blessing. I'm just sorry to admit that I needed something as painful as what we've been through to get my priorities straightened out."

"Thank you, Michael. I'm glad you want to get some counseling with me. I think that will help me feel less insecure. But you should get back to bed, it must be really late. You're going to be exhausted at work tomorrow."

"I'm not going to work tomorrow. We're going to pick out a puppy, remember? Why are you out here in the dark? Aren't you cold?" He pulled her closer as a fresh wave of tears washed over her.

When her emotions settled down, she said quietly, "This is where Heathcliff and I used to sit at night when I needed to pray about something really serious."

"Well, then, why don't we pray right now?"

"Really? Do you mean it?" She smiled up at him with tears still glistening on her eyelashes in the moonlight.

"Of course I mean it. It's about time we prayed together, don't you think?" And with one arm around Juliet's shoulders and his hand holding hers, Michael began to pray.